"Don't make threats, litt[...] enough to back them up." [...] [...] was no point in going easy on [...]

"This is a nice horse," Flores said.

"Yes, he is."

"Be a shame if something happened to him."

Flores didn't have a chance to move. Clint grabbed him by the front of the shirt with his left hand, bunched it up, and lifted the man off his feet, then drew his gun with his right hand. He put the barrel under Flores's chin. "If anything happens to my horse, I won't hesitate. I'll just blow your head off. You got that?"

Flores tried his best to nod and breathe at the same time, his eyes wide with fear. Clint released him, and let him fall to the floor.

Clint took Eclipse's bridle and walked him out of the barn. Outside he mounted up and rode off.

DON'T MISS THESE
ALL-ACTION WESTERN SERIES
FROM THE BERKLEY PUBLISHING GROUP

THE GUNSMITH *by J. R. Roberts*

Clint Adams was a legend among lawmen, outlaws, and ladies. They called him . . . the Gunsmith.

LONGARM *by Tabor Evans*

The popular long-running series about Deputy U.S. Marshal Custis Long—his life, his loves, his fight for justice.

SLOCUM *by Jake Logan*

Today's longest-running action Western. John Slocum rides a deadly trail of hot blood and cold steel.

BUSHWHACKERS *by B. J. Lanagan*

An action-packed series by the creators of Longarm! The rousing adventures of the most brutal gang of cutthroats ever assembled—Quantrill's Raiders.

DIAMONDBACK *by Guy Brewer*

Dex Yancey is Diamondback, a Southern gentleman turned con man when his brother cheats him out of the family fortune. Ladies love him. Gamblers hate him. But nobody pulls one over on Dex . . .

WILDGUN *by Jack Hanson*

The blazing adventures of mountain man Will Barlow—from the creators of Longarm!

TEXAS TRACKER *by Tom Calhoun*

J.T. Law: the most relentless—and dangerous—manhunter in all Texas. Where sheriffs and posses fail, he's the best man to bring in the most vicious outlaws—for a price.

THE GUNSMITH

380
KENTUCKY SHOWDOWN

J. R. ROBERTS

JOVE BOOKS, NEW YORK

THE BERKLEY PUBLISHING GROUP
Published by the Penguin Group
Penguin Group (USA) Inc.
375 Hudson Street, New York, New York 10014, USA

USA | Canada | UK | Ireland | Australia | New Zealand | India | South Africa | China

Penguin Books Ltd., Registered Offices: 80 Strand, London WC2R 0RL, England
For more information about the Penguin Group, visit penguin.com.

KENTUCKY SHOWDOWN

A Jove Book / published by arrangement with the author

Jove Books are published by The Berkley Publishing Group.
JOVE® is a registered trademark of Penguin Group (USA) Inc.
The "J" design is a trademark of Penguin Group (USA) Inc.

For information, address: The Berkley Publishing Group,
a division of Penguin Group (USA) Inc.,
375 Hudson Street, New York, New York 10014.

ISBN: 978-0-515-15388-0

PUBLISHING HISTORY
Jove mass-market edition / August 2013

PRINTED IN THE UNITED STATES OF AMERICA

10 9 8 7 6 5 4 3 2 1

Cover illustration by Sergio Giovine.

ONE

Clint Adams rode into Louisville, Kentucky, several days before the running of the Kentucky Derby. His friend Ben Canby had a horse he was high on, and had invited Clint to come to the Derby and watch him run—and win.

The town was buzzing as he rode down Main Street. It was his intention to spend the night in town, and then the next morning he'd ride out to Canby's horse farm to see his friend, and his horse.

Clint reined in his own horse, Eclipse, in front of a hotel with a livery stable next to it. Most towns were not usually as accommodating.

"Staying at the hotel?" the middle-aged liveryman asked.

"I haven't checked in yet, but yes."

"Okay," the man said, "they'll add the charge for boarding your horse to your bill."

"How convenient."

"Come for the Derby?"

"As a matter of fact, yes."

"I got a tip for you," the man said.

"Is that a fact?"

"Horse named My Officer. Can't miss."

"I'll keep it in mind."

Clint took his saddlebags and rifle and entered the hotel.

"You're lucky," the clerk said. "Got a few rooms left. By tonight we'll probably be full."

"That's okay," Clint said. "I'll only need the room for one night."

"Very well," the clerk said. "Room five. Enjoy your stay." He handed Clint a key. As he turned to go up the stairs, the clerk asked, "Are you here for the Derby?"

"Yes, I am."

The young man leaned his elbows on the desk and said, "I got a tip for you."

"Is that so?"

The man nodded. "A horse named Little Drama. Can't miss."

"I'll keep that in mind."

Clint went up to his room.

He took the time to wash the trail off his hands, face, and chest, then changed into a fresh shirt and went out to find a place for his supper.

The town was alive with activity, most of which—from the scraps of conversation he could catch—had to do with the Kentucky Derby. Apparently, owners and trainers from all over the country were coming to town for the race, to challenge the locals.

At a small café he found down the street, Clint had a mediocre steak and weak coffee, but managed to get still another tip from the waiter—this time a horse named Be Brave. "Can't miss," the man assured him. So that was three "can't miss" tips he'd gotten since arriving in town just an hour before.

He didn't know the name of Ben Canby's horse. He wondered if it was any of the three he'd gotten the tips on.

After supper he crossed the street to a casino called the Crazy Bull. Inside there was a painting of a bull hanging over the bar, but someone had fiddled with the eyes, making them look appropriately "crazy."

"Beer," he told the bartender.

The casino had gambling, girls, and music, and they were all making noise. Just next to him two cowboys were arguing over the abilities of two horses, one called Awesome Gem and the other Fast Frankie. According to each man, the horse he was touting "couldn't miss." Eventually, they came to blows over the subject. Clint picked up his beer and moved away from the action, leaving it to the bartender to take care of.

Carrying his beer with him, he walked around the spacious interior of the casino. He paused to watch a poker game, a blackjack table, a faro table, a roulette wheel, and a craps table. There was no room for him at any of them, so he simply spent a few moments watching the action, and then moved on.

By the time he got back to the bar, the two arguing cowboys were gone.

"What happened to your friends?" he asked the bartender.

"I convinced them to leave," the brawny man said. "You want another?"

"Sure," Clint said, "one more can't hurt. Might even help me sleep."

Actually, he doubted he was going to have any trouble sleeping. He was pretty tired from the time he'd spent on the trail getting there.

"There ya go," the man said, setting a second beer in front of him.

"You here for the Derby?" the man asked.

"Yes, why?" Clint asked. "You got a tip for me?"

"Hell, no," the bartender said. "What do I know about racehorses?"

TWO

Clint turned over in bed and found himself staring at a woman's naked back. She had short black hair, looked slender, although he seemed to remember breasts that more than filled his hands.

He rolled onto his back and gazed at the ceiling. Slowly, it started to come back to him. He was finishing his second beer in the Crazy Bull when a woman approached him. She was a saloon girl, said her name was Jesse. They talked awhile until she was called away to serve some customers.

"Don't go away," she told him, putting her index finger on his chest. "We're not done."

"We're not?"

"No."

She was in her twenties, had a very pretty face with a wide mouth and bright blue eyes.

"Okay," he agreed. "I'll wait."

"Good."

She turned to go and he said, "Wait."

"Yes?"

"You're not going to give me a tip on a horse, are you?"

"Not me," she said. "What I have in mind has nothing to do with horses."

"Oh . . . good."

She nodded, took a tray of drinks from the bartender, and disappeared into the crowd.

"Another beer?" the bartender asked. "While you're waitin'?"

"Sure," he said, "why not . . ."

The woman moaned, brought him back to the present. She rolled onto her back, and he saw that her breasts were indeed a handful or more, even though the rest of her was quite slender.

She stretched, making her breasts go taut, and then she looked over at him.

"Do you need an engraved invitation?" she asked.

He smiled, leaned over her, and began to kiss her neck, her shoulders, her breasts, her nipples . . . she caressed his head, held him there for a while before allowing him to travel lower.

He kissed her pale, smooth skin down to her navel, inhaled the fragrance of her flesh, which—since she had come with him right after work—included some of the smells of the saloon, but mostly the special blend of her own perspiration and skin.

And then lower, and her smells became more intense, headier. He pressed his nose to her pubic hair, then let his tongue party it until he tasted her wetness . . . and she jumped.

"Yes," she said.

He probed her with his tongue, causing her to writhe and moan. The more he licked, the wetter she became—a combination of his saliva and her juices.

Finally, she began to tremble, and then she was doing

more than writhing and moaning. She was jumping and yelling, all the while reaching for him, raking his back, and laughing.

He mounted her finally, pressed his hard cock to her wetness, and pushed. The night before they had joined violently, but this morning he entered her slowly until he was fully in, then began to move, in and out, while she found his rhythm and rocked with him. They were both able to resist the urge to move faster and their movements became languid, fluid, almost like a dance, and then he was the one trembling and then gasping as he emptied into her . . .

"Why me?" he asked as he watched her get dressed. She sheathed her lovely body in the same dress she'd worn last night, green and low cut.

"Why not you?" she asked. "You're good-looking, almost handsome, clean . . . and a stranger. Will you be staying in town long?"

"For the race," he said, "but I won't be staying in town. I'll be staying on my friend's ranch."

"Which ranch is that?"

"The Canby."

"He's got a horse in the Derby, doesn't he?"

"He does," Clint said, "but I don't know the name."

"Neither do I," she said. "So I guess I haven't heard anybody talking about it."

"I've gotten five or six tips since I arrived," Clint said.

"Well then," Jesse said, "you have five or six horses not to bet on. Cuts down the field."

She slipped on her shoes and then looked at him.

"Thank you for a lovely night."

"It was lovely," he said. "Thank you for picking me out."

"If you come by the casino tonight," she said, "I might just pick you out again."

"Maybe I will."

She started for the door, then turned and said, "I think I was so anxious to get your pants off that I never asked you your name."

He hesitated, then said, "Clint. My name is Clint."

"I'll see you again, Clint."

"Jesse," he said.

She smiled, and slipped out the door.

Outside, Jesse crossed the street and stopped next to a man wearing black, who seemed to be staring into a hardware store window.

"Was I right?" he asked.

"Well," she said, "his name is Clint."

"But is he Clint Adams?"

"He didn't say."

"You were supposed to find out."

She looked at him.

"We got . . . involved in something else," she said.

"Yes, well . . . all right."

"My money?" she asked.

He took his hand from his pocket and handed her a few bills.

"Thank you."

"Thank you, Jesse," he said, and watched her as she walked away.

THREE

Clint checked out of the hotel, got Eclipse from the livery stable, and mounted him. Canby had sent him directions on how to get to his farm from Louisville. Kentucky was amazingly green and he rode at a leisurely pace, in no particular hurry. He thought a bit about Jesse, and the night they'd spent together. It had been odd, the way she'd approached him. Very directly. He'd been approached by women before, but this seemed . . . contrived. Although he had enjoyed the night, he felt sure she'd been put up to it. Maybe somebody had been trying to find out who he was—although all they had to do was check the hotel register. In any case, that was why he had only given her his first name.

When the farm came into view, he was impressed. There were many corrals and outbuildings, and a large, two-story main house. There was also a track that Canby used to train his horses.

Clint rode up to the main house while several men stopped what they were doing to look and see who he was. Since none of them knew him, they simply went back to work.

He dismounted in front of the house, and one of the men came over to him.

"Help ya?" the middle-aged man asked. He was short, bow-legged, had the hands of a man who had worked around horses his whole life.

"I'm looking for Ben Canby."

"The boss is around," the man said. "I'll find him. Who should I tell him—"

"Clint Adams," he said. "Tell him it's Clint Adams."

"Ah," the man said, "the boss said you'd be coming. I'm Ed Donnelly."

"Foreman?" Clint asked, shaking the man's hand.

"Manager," Donnelly said. "Come on. I think the boss is in the barn with Whirlwind."

"Whirlwind?"

"Our Derby horse."

"Oh, well, lead the way, then. I've been anxious to meet Whirlwind."

Donnelly led Clint to the large barn. Inside there were many stalls, some of them inhabited. In the back was the largest stall in the structure, more of a small corral, complete with a door. Inside a man was fussing over a horse's legs.

"That's a three-year-old colt, Ben," Clint said, "not a woman."

Ben Canby looked up and smiled when he saw Clint.

"Clint Adams! By God!"

He came to the edge of the stall and shook hands with his friend.

"So this is the horse, eh?" Clint asked. "Whirlwind?"

"This is him," Canby said. He was a tall, slender man in his fifties who had been working with horses for years. "This the finest animal I've ever trained, Clint. And he's gonna win."

"Really?" Clint asked. "Since I got here, I've had tips on five or six other horses."

"Doesn't matter," Canby said. "My horse is gonna win."

"Is that a tip?"

"No," Canby said, "it's a fact. Eddie, will you finish with his legs?"

"Sure, boss."

"Come on, Clint," Canby said. "Let's go up to the house and have a drink."

"My horse."

"Of course," Canby said, "that beautiful Darley. Too bad he's not three. Eddie?"

"I'll see to him, boss."

"Come on, Clint," Canby said. "I'll also show you your room."

FOUR

Ben Canby was a widower whose wife had died ten years before. He lived alone in the big house, but since the place was spotless, Clint had the feeling there was a woman somewhere.

Clint picked up his saddlebags and rifle on the way into the house. Canby led him to his office, where he poured two glasses of whiskey. He handed one to Clint and then sat behind his desk.

"I'm glad you made it," he said.

"I sent you a telegram telling you I would."

"Sure," Canby said, "but I never know when you're gonna go off on a quest."

"A quest?" Clint asked. "I never go off on quests."

"Well, whatever you call them, then," Canby said, "when people ask you for help and you go running."

"You asked me to come here and I came," Clint reminded him.

"Yes, but I don't need help. I just wanted you to share in my triumph."

"Well," Clint said, "you're lucky I like a good horse race."

"This will be a great horse race. Not just a good one."

"Do you see any competition for your horse?" Clint asked. "How about these?" He reeled off the name of the horses he'd received tips on.

"No, no, none of those," Canby said. "Those are all locals, and they're not in the same class as Whirlwind. No, the competition is coming from out of town."

"Like who?"

"There's a horse coming from the East called Easy Going," Canby said. "Supposed to be undefeated."

"Have you seen the animal?"

"Not yet."

"Anybody else?"

"Only one other that I know about," Canby said. "Coming in from California, named Sunday Song. Also undefeated."

"And your horse?"

"Undefeated in five races," Canby said.

"So three undefeated horses," Clint said. "That does sound like an interesting race. How many horses altogether?"

"About fifteen, I think."

"Big field. Could be some bumping."

"It'll be up to my jockey to make sure that doesn't happen."

"Who's the jockey?"

"The same boy who rode him in his first five races," Canby said. "You'll be meeting him." He put his empty glass on the desk. "Let me show you to your room. You can clean up before we eat lunch."

"Who's making lunch?" Clint asked, following Canby into the hall.

"I have a cook, Clint," he said. "She makes breakfast, lunch, and dinner, and she's good. And I've already told her about your coffee."

"Warned her, you mean."

"That's right."

He led Clint through the house and up to the second floor.

"Does she clean, too?" he asked. "This place is pretty clean."

"I've got a girl who comes from town to do that," Canby said.

They walked past several doors until Canby stopped and said, "This is your room."

Clint went into the room. It was larger and more expensively furnished than most hotel rooms he'd ever been in.

"This'll do," he said to Canby.

The man laughed and said, "Water on the dresser. Come on down when you've cleaned up."

"Okay."

"And Clint . . . I'm glad you're here. You're gonna see something amazing."

"I'm looking forward to it."

Canby left Clint to freshen up, closing the door as he went.

Ed Donnelly had just finished unsaddling Eclipse when a man in black entered the barn.

"Was that him?" the man asked.

"It was him," Donnelly said.

"You're sure?"

"He introduced himself."

"He gonna stay awhile?"

"Looks like."

The man nodded, handed Donnelly some money, and then left the barn.

FIVE

Clint washed his face and hands, but wore the same clothes as he went down for lunch. He found Canby seated at the head of a long table in the dining room, alone.

"Ah, just in time," Canby said. "Elena is about to come out with lunch."

Instead of sitting at the other end, Clint pulled up a chair to Canby's right and sat down.

As he did, the door to the kitchen opened and a woman in her fifties came out, carrying plates of food. She set them down in front of the men without a word, and went back to the kitchen, only to reappear with a bottle of whiskey, and a pitcher of water. Clint noticed there was already a glass for each on the table in front of them.

"Thank you, Elena."

The woman nodded and left.

Clint looked at his plate. On it was a perfectly prepared half a chicken, with vegetables.

"Don't worry," Canby said. "Steak for supper."

"This is fine," Clint said. "He picked up a piece and bit into it. "In fact, it's great."

"Yeah," Canby said, picking up his own, "everything Elena cooks is."

As they ate, Clint asked, "When do I get a chance to see your horse run?"

"I'm gonna work him tomorrow morning," Canby said. "Just to keep him loose. You'll see him then."

"Do you know the trainers of the other undefeated horses?"

"I didn't know them until they got here. There was a dinner for all the owners and trainers. We met then."

"What about Whirlwind?" Clint asked. "Does he have an owner?"

"That'd be me," Canby said. "Owner and trainer."

"And the others?"

"They all have separate owners and trainers."

"Where are they all staying?"

"Various hotels and horse farms in the area," Canby said.

"Are there enough farms to accommodate them all?"

"In Kentucky?" Canby asked with a laugh. "Dozens."

"Have you watched any of the other horses train?" Clint asked.

"No need."

"Why not?"

"I have the best horse."

"How can you be so sure, Ben?"

"Clint," Canby said, "I've been around horses all my life. I know when I've got a good one. And I've got a great one."

"How great?" Clint asked.

"I'd put him up against your Eclipse."

"Whoa."

"I would," Canby said, "and I know what your horse can do. I wouldn't put Whirlwind up against him on the trail, but on the racetrack I'd put my horse up against any other."

"Well," Clint said, "that's impressive."

"You'll be even more impressed once you've seen him run," Canby said.

"What are the odds?"

"So far we're six-to-one."

"Who's favored?"

"The other two horses I told you about," Canby said, "Easy Going and Sunday Song."

"Why aren't you favored? You're local."

"That might be working against me," Canby said. "The other two horses have beaten animals from all over the country—the world, even. Whirlwind has only beaten local competition."

"Why haven't you traveled with him?"

"I could have taken him east, run against Easy Going, or west and run against Sunday Song, but if he'd beaten them, then what?"

"Then you wouldn't be six-to-one," Clint said. "You'd be favored."

"That's right."

"Oh, I see. You're going to make a bet."

Canby smiled.

"A very big bet," he said, "and I'd advise you to do the same."

"I might," Clint said. "After I've seen him run."

After lunch, Canby walked Clint around the grounds, introduced him to a few more employees—a groundskeeper, a groom, a vet.

"You keep your own vet around?" Clint asked.

"Oh yeah," Canby said, "and I pay him enough that he doesn't have to have any other patients, just Whirlwind."

"You must be paying him a lot."

"It's worth it, believe me," Canby said.

"You've got other horses."

"Some," Canby said. "He looks after them, too, but none of them can hold a candle to Whirlwind. You'll see, Clint. In the morning, you'll see."

"I've got an idea," Clint said.

"What?"

"Let Eclipse run with your horse tomorrow."

"Are you serious?"

"I just want to see him with another horse at his throatlatch."

"Your monster will give him a run for his money, that's for sure. But I don't want to tire him out."

"No, no," Clint said, "I'll just run with him."

"You're gonna ride?"

"Why not?" Clint said. "It's my horse."

Canby thought it over, then said, "Okay, but early. Six a.m."

"I'll be ready," Clint said. "I'll go out to your stable now and check on my horse."

"Supper will be at seven," Canby said. "I've got some things to do 'til then, so I'll see you at the table."

"Okay," Clint said. "Steak, right?"

"Like I promised," Canby said, "steak."

SIX

Clint went to the stables to check on Eclipse. The big Darley was standing easy. He'd been properly brushed and fed. Clint inspected his legs, just to be sure.

While he was looking over the horse, somebody walked into the stable carrying a couple of buckets. When the person put the buckets down and then straightened up, Clint saw that it was a woman.

"Oh," she said, surprised, "I didn't see you there."

"You surprised me, too."

"That big boy yours?" she asked, indicating Eclipse.

"He is."

"He's magnificent."

"He is that," Clint said. "I've met a bunch of people today, but not you."

"I'm Alicia," she said. "I'm a groom."

"I thought I met the groom."

"No," she said, "I'm the groom. Whirlwind's groom."

"Then who was the man I met?"

"Must have been Frank."

"Yeah, that's right."

"He thinks he's Whirlwind's groom."

"Well, so does Ben, then, because that was how he introduced Frank to me."

"I take care of him," she insisted. "Who are you?"

"I'm a friend of Ben's," he said. "My name's Clint Adams."

"Oh, yeah ," she said, "the Gunsmith. He talks about you."

She took her hat off, and suddenly a tangle of black hair fell to her shoulders. Clint saw that she was probably just this side of thirty, fairly tall, and sturdily built. She used one hand to shake out her hair, then tossed her hat aside.

"Well, I can look after your horse, too, while you're here," she said. "He deserves the best."

"Did you rub him down?" Clint asked.

"I did," she said. "Eddie started, but then I came in and took over. Eddie's the manager around here—he's no groom."

"He let you touch him?" Clint asked. "He doesn't take to a lot of people."

"Watch," she said. She walked to the stall, went inside, and spoke softly to Eclipse. When she touched his nose, he didn't pull away, and then she stroked his neck.

"See?" she asked. "We get along."

"That's good," Clint said. "I appreciate it."

"I'm gonna see to Whirlwind now," she said, coming out of Eclipse's stall.

"Ben told me he's going to work him tomorrow."

"I know," she said, "in the morning."

"Eclipse is going go run with him."

"What?"

"That's right," Clint said. "Ben wants to show off his three-year-old to me, so I thought I'd be able to see better if I was riding alongside him."

"But . . . your horse will run him into the ground," she complained.

"I'm not going to do that," Clint said. "We're just going to run alongside him. I want to get a close-up look."

"Well, if that's all you're gonna do . . ."

"I promise," Clint said. "I'm not going to do anything to hurt Whirlwind's chances in the Derby."

"Well," she said, "I'll take good care of both of them."

"I believe you will," Clint said. "I didn't see you at lunch. Will I be seeing you at supper?"

"You probably will," she said.

"Good," he said. "We can talk more then."

"I'll look forward to it."

Clint left the barn, feeling fairly sure Eclipse was in good hands.

SEVEN

Daniel Farnsworth watched carefully as his groom walked his three-year-old, Easy Going, around the corral.

"What do you think, Mr. Farnsworth?" his trainer, Seamus Callaghan, asked. "How's he look?"

"He looks damn good, Seamus," Farnsworth said. "Take him back in."

Callaghan waved to the groom, who immediately walked the horse back into the stables.

"You still intend to work him before the Derby?" Farnsworth asked.

"Just a light workout, boss," Callaghan said. "I want to keep him loose."

"Have you seen Sunday Song since he arrived?"

"No, I ain't," Callaghan admitted.

"Well, I have," Farnsworth said. "He's looking damn good. Too good."

"Don't worry, boss," Callaghan said. "Easy Going is in the best shape of his life."

Farnsworth, a businessman who had entered the

horse-racing world only five years before, looked his trainer
over. While he himself was sixty, and wore three-piece suits
every day, the trainer—in his fifties—always looked as if
he'd slept in his clothes—in the barn. Maybe that was good,
that he looked like he spent all his time in the barn with his
horses. So far, Callaghan had been very good at his job,
training three champions for Farnsworth. But this horse,
Easy Going, was easily the best horse they'd ever had. Farnsworth affectionately called the animal "Big Red," for the
color of his coat.

Farnsworth had actually found the trainer in Ireland and
brought him over to condition his horses.

"I pay you a lot of money to make sure Big Red is in top
condition, Seamus."

"I know you do, sir," Callaghan said. "Don't you worry.
Yer money's not goin' to waste. I'm doin' my best work with
this horse."

Farnsworth turned and looked at the house he'd rented,
along with the stables and the corral. Behind the house was
a half-mile racetrack that had not been used in a while.
Farnsworth had paid to have the track redone, so it would
be in condition for his horse to run on safely.

"All right," Farnsworth said, "I'll be in the house if you
need me."

"Yes, sir."

"Just remember," the businessman said, "it's not only the
race and the purse that's at stake. I'm going to be making a
sizable bet on Big Red."

"I understand that, boss," Callaghan said. "Don't worry,
he'll be ready."

"He better be."

Callaghan watched his boss walk up to the house, then
turned and went into the barn to examine Easy Going again,
just to make sure.

* * *

A few miles away, at the Two Chimneys Farm, two men were also standing, watching a horse, but these men were of comparable age, mid-forties. One was William Kingston, the owner of Sunday Song, and the other was Ollie Shoemaker, one of the finest trainers in the Thoroughbred racing world. He'd been training horses in the United States for twenty years, had trained half a dozen champions. He had already won two Kentucky Derbies.

Sunday Song was standing still, the groom holding his reins. The animal knew he was being inspected.

"Look at him, Ollie," Kingston said.

"I am, boss," Shoemaker said. "He looks great."

"He is great," Kingston said.

"He's gonna be my third Derby champ."

"And mine," Kingston said. "We're going to be the greatest owner-trainer combination in racing history."

"Not to mention rider."

The jockey was to be Lorenzo Capp, who had ridden all of their champions already. The little black man was considered to be one of the best, if not the best jockey in the sport.

"He's gonna be here tomorrow, right?" Kingston asked.

"Yeah, boss," Shoemaker said, "he'll work the horse in the morning."

"You think the others are working their animals before the race?"

"If I know Callaghan—and I think I do—he will be."

"We're lucky Two Chimneys was available for training," Kingston said. "Best training track I've ever seen."

"That's right," Callaghan said. "And only the best for Sunday Song."

"Come on," Kingston said, putting his arm around his trainer, "let's go and get something to eat."

EIGHT

When Clint came to the table for supper, Ben Canby was already there.

"You don't miss many meals, do you, Ben?"

"Do I look like I miss any meals?" Canby asked. "I'm sixty-five years old, Clint, but I still have the same strength I did when I was forty. I keep myself well fed, and healthy. And yeah, ever since Elena came here to cook for us, I don't miss any meals."

"By the way," Clint said, taking his seat, "I met somebody else today, somebody you didn't introduce me to."

"Who's that?"

"Girl named Alicia."

"Oh," Canby said, "Alicia."

"Yeah," Clint said. "She looks like she has a good hand with horses. With Eclipse anyway."

"The groom I introduced you to?"

"Frank?"

"Right," Canby said, "Frank Dunlap. Well, Alicia's his daughter."

"She told me she was Whirlwind's groom."

"Well, maybe she is," Canby said. "I mean, Frank's the groom, but he's training Alicia for the job."

"Seems to me she thinks she has the job already."

"Yeah, well, that's Alicia."

"She said she might come to supper."

"Frank and Alicia know they can always come here for their meals," Canby said, "but they rarely do."

At that moment they heard the front door open, and moments later Frank the groom entered the dining room with Alicia. She had cleaned herself up, changed clothes, run a brush through her hair. She was beautiful. Frank Dunlap was also wearing clean clothes, and had combed his hair with a part in the middle. He didn't look happy. Clint had a feeling his daughter had cleaned him up.

"Sorry we're late," Alicia said.

"You better tell Elena you're both here for supper," Canby said.

"I will," Alicia said, "and I'll help her serve." She went into the kitchen.

"Haven't seen you this clean in months, Frank," Canby said.

"Alicia's idea," Frank said, taking a seat. "Can't figure out why, though."

Canby looked at Clint and said, "I think I might know."

Elena and Alicia came out carrying huge platters of food and set them in the center of the table. One was piled high with steaks, cooked to varying degrees, from rare to well done.

The other platters were filled with potatoes, onions, carrots, and rolls.

"Clint," Canby said. "You first."

Clint used his fork to spear a rare steak onto his plate, then followed with the vegetables, and a couple of rolls.

Canby grabbed one of the well-done steaks. Frank also took a rare one, while Alicia's was medium rare.

As they cut into their meat, it looked to Clint as if each steak was cooked perfectly.

"Elena is a genius," Canby said.

"Where'd you find her?" Clint asked.

"In town," he said, "running a small café. When her husband died, I offered her a job, and she took it. She lives here, and cooks for us."

"Lucky you," Clint said.

He put a piece of meat in his mouth, and it also melted there it was so tender. He followed that with bites of potatoes, onions, and carrots, all cooked perfectly. He broke a roll, buttered it, and placed it in his mouth.

Genius was an understatement . . .

Over dinner, Alicia asked, "How long will you be staying, Clint?"

"I'm not sure," Clint said. "I'm here for the Derby, but if you win—"

"*When* we win," Canby said, cutting him off, "Clint will have to stay for the celebration."

"I don't have anyplace to be," Clint said, "so we'll see."

Frank didn't talk, he just shoveled food into his mouth.

"I haven't met the jockey yet," Clint said. "Who is he?"

"He's a good boy," Frank said.

"His name is Davy Flores," Canby said. "He's won races for us in the past, but this is his first Kentucky Derby."

"Did you think about getting someone more experienced?"

"I did," Canby said. "I considered it, but in the end I had to stay loyal to Davy. He knows the horse."

"Whirlwind loves him," Alicia said. "He won't run for anybody else."

"Have you ridden him?" Clint asked.

"Once," she said. "I couldn't get him out of a canter. But he runs like the wind for Davy."

"Where is Davy?" Clint asked.

"He'll be here tomorrow," Canby said, "and he'll spend the next two nights. He lives in town, has a job. I'm the only trainer who uses him. After he wins the Derby, though, I think he'll start getting offers from some of the others."

Frank Dunlap speared another steak, so Clint did the same. They were too good to pass up.

Alicia stopped at one, while Canby also reached for a second.

"I'm going to go into the kitchen and help Elena," Alicia said. "I'll see you later."

She spoke as if addressing the table in general, but Canby knew she actually meant the comment for Clint.

Alicia walked into the kitchen while the three men piled their plates high with more meat and vegetables.

NINE

The man in black knocked on the door of the house. When the door was opened to him by a middle-aged man, the visitor said, "I'm here to see him."

"Come this way."

He followed the middle-aged man down a long hall to an office, where he entered and sat in front of a desk.

"What do you have for me?" the man behind the desk asked.

"Confirmation, I suppose," the man in black said. "It seems to be Clint Adams."

"So what's he doin' here?"

"From what I hear, him and Canby are friends."

"That's it?"

The man in black shrugged.

"Keep lookin'," the man behind the desk said. "I want to know more."

The man in black shrugged and said, "As long as you pay the freight."

The man behind the desk opened a drawer, took out an

envelope filled with cash, and tossed it over to the man in black. It landed in his lap.

"I'm payin' the freight," he said.

The other man picked up the envelope and said, "You're the boss."

"Yes," the man behind the desk said, "I am."

The man in black turned and left.

Moments later, the man who had answered the door entered.

"Do we really need him?" he asked.

"I think we do, Gage," the man behind the desk said. "I think we do. Especially if Canby's guest turns out to be the Gunsmith."

"When will we know for sure?" Gage asked.

"Soon," the other man said. "Soon."

"Before the race?"

"We definitely need to know before the race," the man said. "Blacker will get it done."

"Blacker," Gage said, shaking his head. "What came first for him, the clothes or the name?"

"It doesn't really matter," the other man said, "does it?"

TEN

Clint was on the front porch when the door opened and Canby came out. He was carrying two cigars.

"Care for one?"

"Sure," Clint said, accepting, "why not?"

Canby scratched a lucifer to life and they lit both cigars with it.

"Alicia's interested in you," Canby said. "I've never seen her look the way she did tonight."

"Don't worry," Clint said.

"I'm not worried," Canby said. "You could do worse. But you'll have to be careful of Frank."

"Is he protective of her?" Clint asked. "I couldn't tell at supper. He was too busy eating."

Canby laughed.

"Frank doesn't know what's happening," he said.

"And you do?"

"Oh yeah," Canby said. "Alicia's twenty-two, Clint. She's a woman."

"I thought she was older."

"She just looks older," Canby said. "But twenty-two is a full-grown woman. And she knows what she wants."

"I didn't come here for trouble, Ben," Clint said.

"Maybe not," Canby said, "but you've got some . . . the female kind."

"That may be the worst kind."

They smoked their cigars, and then Canby said good night and went back inside. Frank Dunlap had already left. That meant that Alicia was still inside, supposedly helping Elena clean up.

Clint was thinking he should have gone up to his room when the door opened again and Alicia came out.

"Oh," she said. "I didn't know you were out here."

Since her hair looked freshly brushed, he doubted that was true.

"I'm headed home," she said.

"Where's that?"

"Bunkhouse in the back," she said. "We all share it. My dad, Eddie, some of the others."

"You sleep in the bunkhouse with the men?"

She smiled and said, "They treat me like one of the guys."

"Is that the way you want to be treated?"

"By them," she said, "yes."

They stared at each other for a few moments, then she broke the silence and said, "I'll be checking the horses before I turn in."

"Okay."

"In the stables."

"Right."

"Alone."

"I understand."

She was beautiful in the moonlight, her hair as black as

the darkness. The skin of her hands and face had been browned by the sun, but he suddenly found himself wondering what the skin beneath her clothes looked like.

"Good night, Clint."

"Good night, Alicia."

As she walked to the stables, he tried to push the thought of her naked body away, but couldn't. Neither could he ignore the invitation, both in her voice and in her eyes.

She was a woman, all right.

And trouble.

Lots of trouble . . .

Alicia checked on Whirlwind first, going into his stall and inspecting him thoroughly to make sure he hadn't done anything to injure himself. She ran her hands up and down his legs, along his flanks, then went to his head and just stroked him for a while.

"You're a good boy," she told him. "You're gonna run their legs off."

She patted him one last time, and left the stall, making sure the door was locked.

She moved into Eclipse's more common open stall, went in alongside him, and patted his flanks, his neck, and then moved to his head. She stroked his nose and spoke to him.

"You better take it easy on my baby tomorrow," she told him. "Just give him a light workout, okay?"

He nodded his big head, as if he understood what she was telling him.

She came out of the stall and saw Clint standing there.

"Oh," she said, "you surprised me . . . again."

"Sorry," he said, "I was coming out to check on Eclipse."

"He's doin' fine," she said. "In fact, I checked on both of them."

"How did you do that exactly?" he asked.

"You really want to know?"

"Well, sure."

She walked up to him.

"Well, first I feel their legs to be sure they're okay."

She crouched down and ran her hands up and down one of Clint's legs, then the other. As she did, she noticed the bulge in his pants.

"Then what?"

"Then I check out their flanks."

She stood, ran her hands over his thighs, and his buttocks. As she did, she leaned against him, feeling his hard cock press up against her.

"And then what?" he said into her hair.

She drew back and looked him in the eyes.

"Then I rub their nose," she said, using two fingers to rub up and down his nose. "Sometimes I kiss them on the nose." She leaned forward and kissed his nose. He put his arms around her and kissed her on the lips. She opened her mouth to him, and he explored her with his tongue.

"Did you really come out here to check on Eclipse?" she asked.

"What do you think?" he asked. "You pretty much invited me out here, right?"

"Right."

"So," he said, "here I am."

She looked around, found an empty stall, and said, "Let's put some hay in here."

Together they collected enough straw to make a bed in the empty stall.

"All right," she said, unbuttoning her shirt.

He unbuttoned his and they peeled them off. Her breasts were full and heavy, with dark nipples. She reached out and ran her hands over his chest. They kissed again, this time pressing their bare skin together. Then he reached for her belt and undid her trousers, pulling them off, pausing only to remove her boots to make it easier for her.

She did the same to him, tossing his pants aside, and they fell onto the bed of hay together, naked and very eager.

"We'll have to be quiet," he said into her ear, "so we don't spook the horses."

"Or anyone else who might hear us," she whispered back to him.

ELEVEN

The door to Ben Canby's bedroom opened and Elena slipped in.

"You're late," he told her.

"It was Alicia," Elena said. "She insisted on helping me clean up."

She came to the bed, then unbelted her robe and dropped it to the floor. At fifty-five, she was still a lovely woman. She pulled the covers from his naked body, and saw that his cock was hard. At sixty-five, he was still a virile man.

She got on the bed with him, stroked his hard penis, then mounted him and took him inside.

"Take it easy on me," he said. "I'm an old man, remember?"

"Well," she said, "I am not an old woman, not yet anyway, so I am not going to take it too easy."

"Okay, then," he said, putting his hands on her hips. "Okay. I'm with you."

She smiled, pressed her hands down on his chest, and began to ride him . . .

* * *

Clint got Alicia on her back, began to kiss her body, lingering at her lovely, round breasts, licking the smooth skin and her dark aureoles before nibbling on her nipples with his teeth.

She gasped and cradled his head, but he didn't linger there longer. He worked his way down until his face was buried in her crotch, and then went to work on her with his lips and tongue. She grew so wet his face became soaked with her, and his nose filled with her scent, inflaming him even more. Finally, he couldn't wait any longer. He mounted her, spread her legs wide apart, and drove into her. She gasped and clung to him, using her arms and her legs. He began to move inside her. There wasn't much give in the hay beneath them, not like a mattress would have given her. Because of that, his penetration of her was complete. Each time he thrust into her, she gasped again, or grunted, but never in pain, only from pleasure.

"Oh, yes, yes," she said into his ear. They were still trying to stay quiet so no one would hear them. The horses nickered, maybe more from the smells than the sounds. Luckily, Eclipse was a gelding, but the young colt might have detected what was happening. He shifted in his stall, but did not seem to be in any discomfort. They could only hear him, not see him, so they didn't know that his young nostrils were flaring.

Soon they were both grunting and groaning as the sounds of flesh on flesh filled the barn . . .

Canby stood at the window, looking down at the barn, saw the light burning.

"Alicia must be in with the horses," he said.

"Not only the horses," Elena said from the bed.

He turned and looked at her. She held the covers to her,

but one breast remained bare. Her long hair fell to her shoulders. She had worked at the house three months before they had sex the first time. In the past two years, she'd come to him most nights. They never talked about getting married.

"What do you mean?"

"What do you think I mean?" she asked. "You saw how she was looking at Clint."

"But I warned him."

She laughed.

"You have been dealing with too many geldings," she told him. "Come back to bed."

TWELVE

When Clint woke up the next morning, the skin on his back was chafed from the hay. He had left Alicia lying there when they were finished, looking beautiful in the light from the lamp. By the time he got back to his room and looked out his window, the barn was dark.

He rose early, washed up, and went downstairs. No breakfast yet. First they had to work the horse.

When he got out to the corral, Canby was walking Whirlwind around, already saddled.

"I was about to send somebody to wake you," Canby said.

"I'm ready," Clint said. "I'll get Eclipse saddled."

"You gonna put that big McClellan saddle on him?"

"What else?"

Clint looked at Whirlwind, who was wearing a racing saddle that looked like a postage stamp.

"Where's your jockey?" Clint asked.

"He'll be here," Canby said. "Bring out your horse."

Clint went into the barn, paused to look at the hay-filled stall he and Alicia had used the night before. Then he walked to Eclipse's stall, backed the big gelding out, and saddled him.

When he came out with the big Darley, there was a smaller man standing by Ben Canby, and Alicia was standing off to one side. She gave Clint a shy glance, then looked away.

"Clint," Canby said, "this is my jockey, Davy Flores."

Clint shook hands with the diminutive man, who eyed Eclipse and asked, "Who's this?"

"This is Eclipse."

"Wow," Davy said, "I've never ridden a horse this size."

"That's because they don't race horses this size," Clint said.

Davy looked at Canby.

"Am I supposed to outrun this monster?"

"No," Canby said, "Clint is just gonna run along with you. He wants a close look at Whirlwind."

"Well, okay," Flores said.

Canby gave Davy a leg up onto Whirlwind, then walked over and mounted his own mare.

"We'll ride to the track," he said.

"Suits me," Clint said. "Is Alicia coming?"

"She wants to see this," Canby said. "She'll walk."

Clint rode over to her and reached his hand down.

"Come on," he said, "I'll give you a ride."

He hauled her up behind him, and she immediately pressed her breasts into his back and wrapped her arms around him.

"You should know something," she whispered into his ear.

"What's that?" he asked quietly.

"Davy Flores is in love with me," she said. "And he's mean."

"I'll watch out for the little guy," he said. "What about you?"

"What about me?"

"Are you in love with him?"

"No," she said. "He's too . . . small."

Clint had met a lot of small men with big chips on their shoulders. Davy Flores hadn't struck him that way, but then they'd only had time to shake hands.

They rode over to the training track and Clint lowered Alicia to the ground. Canby rode over to sit beside Clint.

"I only want him to go six furlongs," the trainer said.

"Okay," Clint said.

"Don't press him, Clint," Canby said, "just ride alongside him."

"Don't worry," Clint said, "I won't hurt your little horse."

He rode onto the track, where Davy Flores already had Whirlwind prancing about. When Clint rode up alongside them, the smaller man looked up at him.

"Be careful with that big horse," Davy said.

"Don't worry," Clint said, "we won't step on you."

Davy Flores did not take that as a joke. In fact, his face got red.

"I just meant don't get in my way," the jockey said. "Whirlwind is the star. Got it?"

"I got it," Clint said. "Whirlwind is the star. So where do we start from?"

"Follow me."

Whirlwind led the way to the starting point. Canby sat his horse off to one side, holding a stopwatch in his hand.

"The boss will call it," Davy said.

"I won't start 'til you do," Clint promised.

So they sat at the starting point, both watching Canby, waiting for him to call for the start.

"Go!" the trainer said, clicking his watch.

THIRTEEN

A few miles away, two men were watching Easy Going work around the track. Daniel Farnsworth and Seamus Callaghan watched as their jockey, Tommy Baze, put their horse through his paces.

"He's movin' beautifully," Callaghan said.

"He sure is," Farnsworth said. "These locals don't have a chance. Our only competition is Sunday Song."

The two horses—Easy Going and Sunday Song—had managed to avoid each other up to now. The Derby would be their first race against each other, and they were getting all the coverage.

"Don't worry," Callaghan said. "We'll beat him."

"We'd better," Farnsworth said.

At Two Chimneys, owner William Kingston and trainer Ollie Shoemaker were watching Lorenzo Capp run Sunday Song around the best training track in Kentucky.

"Like a freight train," Kingston said. "He's gonna go

around that Derby track like a train, leaving everything in his wake, gasping."

"Yes, sir."

Kingston looked at his trainer and said, "You don't sound as sure as I do, Ollie."

"That Easy Going," Ollie said, "is some horse, Mr. Kingston. And there's—"

"I know that, Ollie," Kingston said. "But so is Sunday Song. In fact, Sunday Song is better. If you don't know that, then maybe I need another trainer."

They had been together a long time, but that didn't stop Kingston from threatening to fire Ollie every time they didn't see eye to eye.

"Well, boss," Ollie said, "I've also been hearing some talk about a local horse."

"What local horse?"

"They call him Whirlwind."

"I never heard of him. Is he entered in the Derby?" Kingston asked.

"Yes, sir."

"Who trains him?"

"A local trainer named Canby, Ben Canby."

"I never heard of him either," Kingston said. "Ollie, I'm not going to worry about a horse I never heard of that's being trained by a man I never heard of. I've got enough to worry about," Kingston said.

"Yes, sir."

"Just see to our horse," Kingston said.

"Yes, sir."

Kingston watched Shoemaker run to meet the jockey and the horse. For a moment he thought he saw a glint of light on a hillside beyond the training track, but then he told himself he was being too paranoid.

He turned to go into the house.

* * *

In truth, there was somebody watching Sunday Song work, someone watching Easy Going, and even someone with a stopwatch watching Davy Flores put Whirlwind through his paces.

Not to mention the Gunsmith riding on that big gelding of his . . .

Clint let Davy take Whirlwind out, holding Eclipse back a bit. It didn't take him very long to realize that he could have run the little three-year-old down anytime he wanted to—but he didn't want to.

He ran along behind the animal, watching him, liking the ease with which he moved, his fluidity, the muscles bunching beneath his hide, his tail swishing as he ran. Clint wondered if that would happen during the race.

After a couple of furlongs he urged Eclipse on and they caught up to the colt, going stride for stride with him. He could see that Whirlwind knew Eclipse was there, and he increased his pace a bit, even as the jockey tried to restrain him. With that kind of competitive spirit, the horse would do well in the Kentucky Derby, where he would only be facing other three-year-old colts.

Clint eased off on Eclipse, allowing Whirlwind to pull ahead, and he simply paced him from behind for the rest of the workout. When it was over, Davy slowed the animal down, but kept him moving, to cool him down.

Clint rode over to where Canby was sitting his own horse. Alicia was standing off to the side. She was still avoiding his gaze. He wondered how a woman who had done the things she'd done with him the night before could act so shy the next morning.

"Well?" Canby asked. "What do you think?"

Clint suddenly realized that this was why his friend had

invited him. Not to watch the Derby, but to see the horse and give his opinion.

"I think he's going to do well, Ben."

"You see the way the jockey had to hold him back when Eclipse ran up alongside him?"

"I did," Clint said. "He's not going to like having other horses around him. Is Davy going to take him right to the front?"

"You bet he is," Canby said. "I got the fastest horse in Kentucky, Clint—and he can stay. Maybe not with Eclipse, but with other horses his own age, he can stay."

"Staying" meant that the horse could last the distance with no problem. The Derby was a mile and a quarter, and many horses who were fast at six furlongs—a furlong being an eighth of a mile—could not last at longer distances.

"So," Canby asked, "you gonna bet on him?"

"I'll put something down on your horse, Ben."

They watched as Davy got off the horse and walked him for a while, and then Alicia ran out and took the horse from him.

They exchanged some words, and then Davy Flores walked over to where his boss and Clint were sitting their horses.

"I think I coulda took you, Adams," the jockey said. "Whirlwind made a move when you came to us."

"He did," Clint said. "I noticed."

"We pulled away," Flores went on. "I had to stop him from hitting top speed."

"I know," Clint said.

"We could've took you and your big horse."

Clint looked at Canby. He didn't want to say anything that would hurt his friend's feelings, but he wanted to tell the little jockey off. Eclipse could have run past Whirlwind anytime he wanted to. Clint knew it, so did Canby, so did Alicia . . .

And so did Flores.

FOURTEEN

The man in black—whose name happened to be Blacker—clicked his stopwatch and checked the time. Not especially fast, but then they had not really pushed the three-year-old. He'd shown some heart, though, when the big gelding pulled up alongside him. Blacker knew that everyone was either betting on the horse from the East or the horse from California. He also knew that a lot of locals were touting their horses. But a "local" himself—though not specifically from the Kentucky area—Blacker had some interest in this horse called Whirlwind, and his little-known trainer.

Clint Adams, on the other hand, was well known, and appeared to be a friend of Ben Canby's. If Adams was here to lay his money down—or even just to offer support—then maybe there was something to this little horse.

And maybe something was going to have to be done about him.

About both of them.

Blacker put his spyglass and watch away, mounted up, and rode off. He had to report to his boss.

* * *

Clint had also seen a glint of light that morning, but did not dismiss it lightly.

"Ben?"

"Yeah?"

"Somebody's been watching."

"Where?" Canby started to look around.

"From that hill," Clint said, pointing.

Canby looked.

"Still there?"

"No," Clint said, "I think he's gone."

Canby looked at Clint.

"Somebody's worried about us."

"You been talking this horse up?"

"Nope," Canby said, "fact is, I ain't said a word to anybody."

"Well then, somebody's paying attention," Clint said. "Or maybe somebody's just checking out all the competition."

"I think I'll take a ride up there, see what I can see," Clint said.

"Okay," Canby said. "Let me know."

Clint rode Eclipse up onto the rise where he'd seen the glint of light, probably a pair of binoculars or a spyglass, as someone watched Whirlwind work out. Of course, being who he was, he had to consider the possibility that they were watching him. They could have recognized him in town, and were wondering what he was up to. He probably should have checked in with the local law when he arrived, but he'd figured his time in town was going to be limited, since he was coming out to Canby's place.

He dismounted and checked the ground. He found the tracks of a single horse, and the boot prints of the rider. The man had stood here and, judging from the marks on the ground, might even have gone down on one knee to have a look through his glass. There were no cigarette butts to indicate he'd smoked while he was there, or any evidence of tobacco juice he might have spit. The area was clean.

He turned when he heard a horse approaching, wondering if the culprit was coming back. He grabbed Eclipse's reins and prepared for a confrontation, but when the rider appeared, it was Alicia, riding a horse Clint had seen in the barn earlier.

"What did you find?" she asked.

"Nothing. What did you think I'd find?"

"I don't know," she said, getting off her horse. "The boss told me you rode up here. I just wanted to make sure you were all right."

"I'm fine. I just took a look around."

"And?"

"One man, one horse," Clint said. "He stood about here and watched."

"Watched what?"

"Either me, or Whirlwind's workout."

"A spy."

"Maybe."

"Why would somebody be watching you?"

"Because of who I am."

"You mean that Gunsmith business?"

"Yes, that Gunsmith business."

She eyed him quizzically and asked, "Is that for real?"

"Is what for real?"

"All that fast gun stuff?" she asked. "I mean, that stuff about you . . . killing people?"

"Are you asking me if I've killed people?"

"Well . . . yes."

"I have," he said, "but only when they were trying to kill me."

"Um, how many?"

"I don't keep count, Alicia."

"But . . . a lot?"

"Where's this coming from?" he asked.

"Davy," she said. "He told me that you're . . . a killer."

"Why do you think he told you that?"

"I don't know."

"You told me he's in love with you," he said. "Do you think he suspects something is going on? Maybe he's jealous? Or trying to scare you away from me?"

"But if it's true—"

"You're going to have to decide for yourself what's true and what isn't, Alicia. I can't help you with that."

He mounted Eclipse, then looked down at her.

"Are you coming back down?"

"Not right now," she said. "I think I'll stay up here for a while and do some thinking."

"That sounds like a good idea to me," he said. "I'll tell Ben. You take all the time you need."

He turned Eclipse around and rode him back down toward the training track. He figured he'd spent as much time with Alicia as he was going to.

FIFTEEN

As Blacker entered his boss's office, he saw two stopwatches on the desk. He placed his alongside the others.

"How did the horse look?" his boss asked.

"Like a million dollars," Blacker said. "It ran with the Gunsmith's big gelding. That's a horse with a lot of competitive drive."

His boss nodded thoughtfully.

"How about the others?" Blacker asked.

"As advertised," the boss said.

"Gonna be some race," Blacker said.

"I'm not looking for 'some race,'" the boss said. "I'm looking to make money."

"With a bet?"

"To start."

"How will you bet?"

"I have a couple of days to figure that out," the boss said. "A couple of days to do something."

Blacker laughed.

"You mean we have two days for me to do something," he said.

"True," his boss said, "but I'm the one who will decide what you do."

"Well," Blacker said. "you let me know when you decide. I'll be around."

"What do you plan to do?" Canby asked Clint.

"I thought I'd follow the trail, see where it leads me," Clint said. "Maybe I can find out who was on that hill. And why."

"It's not really important, you know," Canby said. "It just means that somebody recognized Whirlwind as a threat."

"That's one way of looking at it."

"What's another?"

"That they were watching me," Clint said. "I have to find out."

"I can see that," Canby said. "If someone's got it out for you, you wanna know it."

"Right."

"Well," Canby said, "do what you've got to do, Clint. Then come back here."

They were in Canby's house, and when the trainer walked in, Clint explained again what he'd found on the hill. He hadn't said anything about Alicia yet.

"Before I go . . ."

"Yeah?" asked Canby.

"In case I run into him," Clint said, "what can you tell me about the local sheriff?"

"Ted Hackett?" Canby said. "He's a bad checker player, but a pretty good sheriff, I think."

"Can I use your name if I see him?"

"Sure," Canby said. "Tell him you're a friend of mine." The man shrugged. "See what that gets you."

"I will."

Clint turned to leave, still unsure of what to tell Canby about Alicia.

"Clint?"

He turned back.

"Have you seen Alicia?"

"She's up on that hill."

"What is she doin' up there?"

"Thinking."

"About what?"

"A few things," Clint said. "Give her time. She'll be back."

"If you say so."

Clint turned to face the man again.

"What about Davy Flores?"

"What about him?" Canby asked. "He's a good jockey."

"What else?"

"He's a mean man," Canby said. "That small man mean, you know?"

"Dangerous?"

"Only to himself."

Clint nodded.

"Okay," he said. "I'll be back later tonight."

"Watch your back."

"I've been doing that for a long time, Ben," Clint said. "You watch your horse, just in case whoever was watching means him harm."

Canby looked shocked.

"I hadn't thought of that," he said. "I just thought maybe somebody was spying on us. You know, to get some information before making a bet."

"Well, I'm just saying, be careful."

"I'll arm a couple of my men, just in case."

"Good idea," Clint said. "I'll let you know as soon as I find out anything."

SIXTEEN

Clint avoided Alicia and picked up the trail on the other side of the hill. He followed it for a few miles, and then it disappeared. He rode in a circle, trying to pick it up again. He realized then that the rider had hidden his trail, as if he'd expected to be followed.

Somebody knew what he was doing, better than he did. Clint was an able tracker, but not an expert one.

He mounted up and rode for Louisville.

Clint entered the sheriff's office, found the man seated behind a huge desk in a fairly modern-looking office. Gone were the potbellied stove and the wanted posters. There were two deputies standing there, apparently being dressed down by the sheriff.

". . . next time I catch you two goin' at it, you're both fired. Is that understood?"

"Yes, sir," they both said.

"Now get out," the sheriff said. "Go do your jobs."

The two young deputies turned, walked around Clint—one on either side—and went out the door.

"They're young," the sheriff said. "You've got to keep a tight rein on the young."

"Amen," Clint said.

"What can I do for you, Mr. Adams?"

"You know who I am?"

"I know who you are, and when you got to town," the lawman said. "It's my job."

Sheriff Theodore Hackett was in his late fifties, a robust-looking man with ruddy skin tones and sparkling blue eyes.

"I also know that you're friends with Ben Canby."

"I am."

"Ben's good people," Hackett said.

Clint looked around.

"This is a pretty modern-looking office."

"Louisville is thinking about bringing in a police force," Hackett said. I'm tryin' to convince them they don't need one. What can I do for you, Mr. Adams?"

"Somebody's been spying on Ben Canby's place, watching his horse work out," Clint said. "I tracked him for a while, but then lost the trail."

"I'm afraid I'm not much of a tracker," Hackett said. "Besides, spying ain't exactly a crime. What do you want me to do?"

"Nothing," Clint said, "not yet anyway. I just need you to suggest someone who can read sign. I need an expert, because the man I was trailing took steps to cover his trail."

"I see," Hackett said. "Well, the man you want is probably John Sun Horse."

"An Indian?"

"Full-blooded Cherokee."

"That's perfect," Clint said. "Where do I find him?"

Hackett spread his arms and said, "Pick a saloon."

"He's a drunk?"

Hackett thought a moment, then said, "Let's just say he's drunk . . . a lot of the time."

"Is there a particular saloon I should look in?" Clint asked.

Hackett took a piece of paper from his desk and wrote three names on it. He then handed the paper to Clint.

"I suggest you try these three first," he said. "If you don't find him there, you'll just have to start trying the others."

SEVENTEEN

The third saloon Clint entered was called the Buckshot.
It was midday, and the place was not even half full. He
stood just inside the batwing doors and looked around.
At a back table sat an Indian wearing a top hat, staring
into a mug of beer that had about an inch or two left
in it.

Clint walked to the bar and asked the bartender, "Is that
John Sun Horse back there?"

"That's him."

"Is he drunk?"

"Is he awake?" the bartender asked. "If he's awake, he's
drunk."

"Is he always drunk?"

"Only when he's not workin'."

"How often does he work?"

"Hardly ever."

Clint turned and looked at the Indian.

"You gonna try to talk to him?" the bartender asked.

"I am."

"Wait."

The bartender drew two beers and put them on the bar in front of Clint.

"You better take this to him," he said. "He won't even talk to you otherwise."

"Two?"

"One's for you."

"Oh. Thanks."

"Thank me by putting four bits on the bar."

Clint took out the money and set it down, then picked up the two mugs and walked to the back table.

"You look like you can use a fresh one," he said, putting one beer down in front of the Indian.

The man looked up, brown eyes studying Clint from beneath the brim of his worn top hat. He had a thick nose and fleshy mouth, looked to be about thirty-five.

He pushed his empty mug away and wrapped his hand around the full one.

"Mind if I sit?" Clint asked.

Sun Horse shrugged.

Clint sat.

"I have a job for you, Mr. Sun Horse."

"I am John Sun Horse," the man said. "Or just Sun Horse. No 'Mr.'"

"All right, John Sun Horse. I have a job for you."

"Doing what?"

"What I hear you're good at."

Without smiling, Sun Horse said, "Drinking?"

"Tracking."

"Oh, that."

"You are an expert tracker, aren't you?"

"I am." He took two big swallows of the fresh, cold beer. Clint sipped his.

"I need you to pick up a trail that somebody is trying to hide."

"Not an easy thing," Sun Horse said, "especially if your quarry knows what he is doing."

"Apparently he does."

"How do you know?"

Because I can't find the trail."

Sun Horse looked Clint in the eyes.

"Who are you?"

"Clint Adams."

"This is true?" Sun Horse asked without the slightest look of surprise on his face.

"Yes."

"And you want to hire me?"

"Yes."

"Why?"

"I need to find out who was watching me this morning."

"Where?"

"I was out at the Canby place."

"He has a horse entered in the Derby."

"Yes."

Sun Horse leaned forward then, the first look of interest in his eyes.

"Can you tell me if the horse is going to win?" the Cherokee asked.

"No."

Sun Horse leaned back, sipped his beer again.

"But I can tell you the horse is in fine shape," Clint said.

"So are the others," Sun Horse said. "That doesn't help me make a bet."

"Well," Clint said, "maybe if you take the job, you'll be able to find something out that will help you."

Sun Horse leaned forward again.

"Are you sure your quarry was watching you?" he asked. "Or the horse?"

"That is what I want to find out."

Sun Horse sat back again. Despite what the bartender had said, John Sun Horse did not appear to be drunk.

"Will you take the job?"

"You will pay me?"

"I will."

"How much?"

"Enough to make a healthy bet on the Kentucky Derby."

Very deliberately John Sun Horse pushed the remainder of the beer away.

"You're not going to finish that?" Clint asked.

Sun Horse looked at him and said, "I never drink when I am working."

EIGHTEEN

They went to a nearby livery stable to pick up John Sun Horse's swaybacked mare.

"This is your horse?" Clint asked.

"Yes."

Clint looked the animal over while Sun Horse tossed a blanket on her back.

"What's wrong with my horse?" the Cherokee asked. "She's a good animal."

"She's kind of long in the tooth," Clint commented. "What is she, about ten years old?"

"She'll do fine," Sun Horse said. "She always has." He affixed a bridle to the horse and then looked at Clint. "Where's your horse?"

"In front of the sheriff's office."

"Well, I am ready."

"Fine," Clint said. "I just hope your horse can keep up."

"Sheba will keep up."

"Sheba?"

Sun Horse stared at him, no sign of humor in his eyes.

"Oh, all right," Clint said. "Come on, Sheba."

* * *

"This is your horse?" Sun Horse asked when they reached Eclipse.

"That's right."

John Sun Horse looked Eclipse over.

"Still think your Sheba can keep up?"

"You just watch."

They both mounted their horses, Clint sitting considerably higher than Sun Horse.

"You lead the way," Sun Horse said.

"Don't you know where the Canby place is?"

"I do," Sun Horse said, "but I do not know where this man who was watching you was standing."

"Good point. But maybe I should take you to the place where I lost his trail."

"I want to see where he was when he was watching you," Sun Horse said. "I want to see his tracks, and his horse's tracks. Then I will be able to recognize them when I see them."

"All right, that makes sense. I'll take the lead."

They rode out of town.

"He was right here," Clint said when they reached the hillside.

John Sun Horse nodded and dismounted. He handed the reins of his horse to Clint, who had to admit that the ten-year-old mare had, indeed, kept up with Eclipse.

Sun Horse walked the area, always looking down, crouching from time to time. Clint thought this was a good way to judge the man's abilities. If he tracked the man to the same point Clint had lost him, then he surely knew what he was doing.

"All right," Sun Horse said, reclaiming his reins and mounting up.

"Want me to take you to the place where I lost him?" Clint asked.

"No," Sun Horse said. "I will track him that far myself."

"Okay," Clint said. "You're the expert."

"That's right," John Sun Horse said with no hint of humor on his stolid face. "I am."

NINETEEN

While John Sun Horse did his work, Clint tried to engage him in conversation, but the Cherokee did not seem to be the talkative type. Clint finally fell silent and remained that way.

Eventually, they came to the place where Clint had lost the trail.

"Here," Sun Horse said. "This is where he tried to cover his trail."

"This is where I lost him, all right."

Sun Horse nodded and slipped from his horse's back. He walked the area, looking at the ground intensely, careful of where he set his moccasin-covered feet.

Finally, he knelt for a long time, swiping lightly at the ground with one hand, then stood and walked back to Clint.

"Your man knows what he is doing," Sun Horse said.

"But you found the trail?"

"Of course," Sun Horse said, mounting up. "That is what you are paying me to do, is it not?"

"It is."

Clint wished the Cherokee would exhibit more expression when he spoke. Part of the time—almost half the time, in fact—he felt the man was pulling his leg.

By late afternoon they were sitting outside the gate of a ranch. There was no fence, just an arch built as an entry to the property. There was no name anywhere.

"Here," John Sun Horse said. "This is where your man went."

"Do you know whose place this is?" Clint asked.

"Yes I do," the Cherokee said.

Clint waited, but when he realized nothing further was forthcoming, he said, "Who?"

"Peter Fontaine."

"And who is Peter Fontaine?"

"A rich man."

"What does he do?"

"He gambles."

"Bets on the horses?"

"Bets on anything," Sun Horse said.

Well, it made sense that such a man would be looking for an edge when it came to betting on the Derby.

"What do you do now?" Sun Horse asked.

"Do you know this Fontaine?"

"I know of him," Sun Horse said. "I do not know him."

So, no introduction there.

"Let's go back to Louisville," Clint said. "I want to talk to the sheriff again."

Sun Horse nodded and turned his horse around.

As they rode into Louisville, Sun Horse asked, "You pay me now?"

"You did your job," Clint said. "I'll pay you now."

Sun Horse reined his horse in. Clint went a few more feet before he realized the man had stopped. He turned and looked at him.

"You mean right here, in the middle of the street?" he asked.

"I do not like the law," Sun Horse said. "I don't want to go to the sheriff's office."

Clint rode back to Sun Horse, reached into his pocket, and pulled out some money. He counted out the amount they had agreed upon into Sun Horse's hand. The Cherokee then nodded and tucked the money away in his war bag.

"If you need Sun Horse again," he said, "I will be in the saloon."

"Which one?" Clint asked.

The Cherokee shrugged and said, "All of them."

Clint watched as the man rode away, then shrugged himself and continued on to the sheriff's office.

Sheriff Ted Hackett looked at Clint as he came in the door.

"Find Sun Horse?"

"I did, thanks."

"He get the job done for you?"

"Yes, he did."

Hackett had been standing at the gun rack when Clint entered. Now he turned and seated himself behind his desk.

"What else can I do for you?"

"Tell me about a man named Fontaine."

"Pete Fontaine?"

"That's the one."

"Pete Fontaine is a man nobody wants to cross," Sheriff Hackett said, "not even the Gunsmith."

"Well," Clint said, "maybe you can elaborate on that for me?"

Hackett opened his bottom drawer and came out with a bottle of whiskey.

"This'll take a drink," he announced.

TWENTY

"Fontaine is a gambler," Hackett said. "And I don't just mean that he plays poker or bets on horses. He gambles with his whole life. And the chances he takes always pay off."

"So he's a businessman."

"Yes," Hackett said, "but he takes that to the next level."

"Is he dangerous?"

"He'll do anything to make money."

"Anything?"

"I mean anything."

"So why would he have a man watching me?" Clint asked. "It was more likely he was watching Whirlwind."

"Is that what Sun Horse found out for you?"

"He tracked the man to the Fontaine ranch."

"Did you talk to Fontaine?"

"No," Clint said, "I wanted to get your take on him first."

"My take," Hackett said, "is that he's always up to something."

"I'll keep that in mind. Thanks."

As Clint walked to the door, Hackett asked, "You gonna go and talk to him now?"

"No," Clint said. "I'm going back to the Canby place first."

"Good," Hackett said. "Talk to Ben about Fontaine."

"Are they friends?"

"They are definitely not friends," the sheriff said.

"I see."

"And be careful if you go to Fontaine's place," Hackett said. "Watch your back. Fontaine employs men who are good with a gun."

"Anybody in particular?" Clint asked.

"Fella named Blacker."

"Never heard of him."

"That's his biggest asset," Hackett said. "Nobody's ever heard of him."

"Okay," Clint said. "Thanks for the information."

"But do me a favor, will you?"

"What's that?"

"Try not to kill anybody in my town," Hackett said. "At least, not until after the Derby."

"I'll give it my best shot."

Blacker entered Peter Fontaine's office. His boss looked up.

"What have you got?"

"Word from town."

"About what?"

"Adams tracked me from the Canby place to here."

"Well, how did that happen?" Fontaine asked. "I thought you hid your trail. I thought you were good at this."

"I did, and I am," Fontaine said, "but he hired John Sun Horse."

"That drunken Indian?"

"That drunken Indian is the best tracker I know of," Blacker said.

"And how did Adams know to hire him?"

"He must have been recommended to him."

"By who?"

Blacker shrugged.

"Could have been anybody in town who knew enough to do it," he said. "Maybe the sheriff."

"All right," Fontaine said. He sat back in his chair. "All right," he said again. "So I should be expecting a visit from Clint Adams."

"Probably."

"When that happens," Fontaine said, "I want you around."

"It's either gonna happen today or tomorrow," Blacker told him.

"Then get yourself a bunk in the bunkhouse," Fontaine said.

"Not without bein' on the payroll."

"I pay you a lot as it is," Fontaine said.

"A little more never hurt."

"Okay," Fontaine said. "You're on the payroll. Tell Quincy to give you a bunk."

"Okay," Blacker said. "Boss."

Fontaine waited for Blacker to leave, then stood up, walked to a sidebar, and poured himself a whiskey. Clint Adams was a famous man. There had to be some way for Fontaine to use that fame to make himself some money. If there was a way, he'd find it, because that was what Pete Fontaine did.

He took any situation, and made money from it.

TWENTY-ONE

Clint returned to the Canby ranch in time for supper. He entered the house, found Canby sitting alone at the table.

"Just in time," Canby told him.

"Let me clean up," Clint said. "I'll be right back."

He went into the kitchen, surprising Elena, who was standing at the stove.

"Can I wash up in here, Elena?"

"Yes, sir," she said. "Go ahead."

Clint washed and dried his hands. "That smells great," he told her.

"It's a roast. I'm glad you got back in time," she said.

"So am I," he said, and went back out to the dining room.

"Where have you been all day?" Canby asked.

"Trying to find the man who was watching us this morning."

"And did you?"

"I think so," Clint said. "I hired a man named John Sun Horse to track him."

"Sun Horse? The drunken Cherokee?"

"He never drinks while he's working."

"What did he find?"

"He tracked the rider to Peter Fontaine's doorstep."

"Fontaine?"

Elena came through the kitchen door carrying the roast, stopped short, apparently when she heard the name. She came forward again, placed the roast on the table, exchanged a look with Canby, and went back to the kitchen.

"What was that about?"

"She worked for Pete Fontaine for a short time."

"What happened?"

"She quit."

"Why?"

"She never said, but we can assume it was nothing good."

"What's your relationship with Fontaine?"

"I hate the sonofabitch."

"Why?"

"I did business with him once or twice, came out on the short end. He's ruthless. Will do anything to make money."

"That's what I heard," Clint said. "So he sent somebody to watch the horse work out."

"He's looking for an edge," Canby said, taking a piece of roast.

"Just to make a bet?" Clint wondered aloud. "Or for some other reason?"

"Like what?" Canby asked.

The kitchen door opened again and Elena came out with a platter of vegetables. She set it on the table and returned to the kitchen.

"I don't know what," Clint said, adding vegetables to his plate. "I thought you would, since you know him."

"I don't know," Canby said. "Who did he send to spy on us?"

"I don't know," Clint said, "but I'm told he has hired guns working for him."

"What do hired guns have to do with the Kentucky Derby?"

"I don't know," Clint said. "Have you ever heard of a man named Blacker?"

"Just Blacker?"

"That's all I have."

"I've never heard—wait. Blacker? Maybe I have heard the name, but I don't know him."

"Your friend, the sheriff, told me Blacker's dangerous."

"Dangerous as you?"

"Hackett said nobody wants to cross Fontaine, not even me."

"Fontaine's not a gunman," Canby said. "So he needs hired guns with him."

"And Blacker is probably the best."

"But you've never heard of him?"

"I haven't heard of every fast gun alive, Ben," Clint said. "Some of them go undiscovered, you know. Just like a bunch of fast horses go unknown."

"Well," Canby said, "after the Derby everyone's gonna know the name 'Whirlwind.' "

"You hope."

"Clint," Canby said, "I get the feeling you haven't been listening to me. I know my horse is gonna win."

"How much are you going to bet on him, Ben?" Clint asked.

"A lot," Canby said. "Whatever I can raise."

"Wait a minute," Clint said. "You're going to go all in on this?"

"All in," Canby said. "Definitely."

After supper Clint and Canby went out onto the porch with cigars.

"What are you gonna do tomorrow?" Canby asked.

"I'm going to see Fontaine."

"What for?"

"Because I want to know what's going on."

"Don't tell him about Whirlwind," Canby said.

"Ben, I think he knows about Whirlwind."

"I mean, don't tell him what I said about Whirlwind," Canby said. "I mean, that he's definitely gonna win."

"You don't want Fontaine to make a winning bet."

"No, I don't."

"I'll tell you something," Clint said. "If Fontaine is having Whirlwind watched, I'll bet he's having those other horses watched, too."

"Easy Going and Sunday Song?"

"Right, those two. Don't you think one of those two might win?"

"They might," Canby said, "but they ain't."

"How can you be so sure?" Clint asked.

"Clint," Canby said, "I've been around horses all my life. Believe me when I tell you, this one just won't lose."

TWENTY-TWO

In the morning, after breakfast, Clint went to the barn to saddle Eclipse. He was going to ride directly to Fontaine's and confront him.

He was tightening the cinch on the saddle when Davy Flores walked in.

"Good morning," he said.

"What did you do to Alicia?" the little man asked.

"What? I didn't do anything to her."

"She won't talk to me."

"Well," Clint said, "maybe that's because of something you did."

Flores pointed his finger at Clint.

"If you did anything to hurt her—"

"Don't make threats, little man," Clint said. "You're not big enough to back them up." He didn't like Flores, so there was no point in going easy on him.

"This is a nice horse," Flores said.

"Yes, he is."

"Be a shame if something happened to him."

Flores didn't have a chance to move. Clint grabbed him

by the front of the shirt with his left hand, bunched it up, and lifted the man off his feet, then drew his gun with his right. He put the barrel of the gun under the small man's chin.

"If anything happens to my horse, I won't hesitate, I'll just blow your head off. You got that?"

Flores tried his best to nod and breathe at the same time, his eyes wide with fear. Clint released him, let him fall to the floor.

Clint took Eclipse's bridle and walked him out of the barn. Outside he mounted up and rode off.

Clint rode through the gate of Fontaine's place and followed the roads to the front of the house. He dismounted, dropped Eclipse's reins to the ground, knowing the big gelding would not move unless he had to.

He climbed the steps to the porch, then turned to look around. There was not a man in sight. He turned and knocked on the front door. A tall man wearing a white shirt, gray vest, and gray pants opened it. He was about sixty, with a shock of white hair and matching eyebrows.

"Can I help you?"

"I'd like to see Mr. Fontaine."

"Can I say who is calling?"

"Clint Adams."

"And what's this about?"

Clint hesitated, then said, "Tell him it's about money."

"Wait here."

Fontaine looked up as his man, Henry Gage, entered his office.

"Well?"

"He's here," Gage said. "The Gunsmith."

"Did he scare you?"

"No."

"You look scared, Gage."

"Well, what do you want?" Gage asked. "He's the god-damned Gunsmith."

"What did he say he wanted?"

"To talk to you."

"About what?"

"Money."

Fontaine laughed.

"That's smart," Fontaine said. "Okay, show him in, Gage."

TWENTY-THREE

Gage showed Clint into Peter Fontaine's office. The walls were lined with books. The man himself sat behind a huge cherrywood desk. He appeared to be in his late forties, and even at home behind his own desk, he was wearing an expensive suit and tie. Or was he expecting company?

"Mr. Adams," he said, standing. "Have a seat."

"Were you expecting me?" Clint asked.

"Not at all," Fontaine said, "but I've heard of you, of course."

Clint shook Fontaine's proffered hand and sat down.

"Can I offer you a drink?"

"Too early," Clint said.

"Coffee?"

"No, thanks."

"Well then . . ." Fontaine sat back down. "Perhaps you'd like to tell me what I can do for you?"

"I'm wondering what your interest is in a horse called Whirlwind."

"Whirlwind? I hear he's a prime candidate for the Derby. For a local horse, I mean."

"Do you think he can win?"

"I'm sure I don't know," Fontaine said. "Not at this point. There are a couple of good horses coming in from out of town."

"Yes, I've heard of them," I said. "But you had a man watching Whirlwind work out yesterday."

"Did I?"

"I tracked him from the Canby place to here," Clint said. "You're not going to deny he came here, are you?"

Fontaine seemed to consider the question for a moment, then shrugged and said, "No, why should I deny it? The fact is, I had someone watching all three of the horses."

"Easy Going and Sunday Song?"

"Yes," Fontaine said. "I feel these are the three with the best chance to win."

"Have you decided where to place your bet yet?"

"Not yet," he said. "We still have a couple of days, however."

"Yes, we do."

"But you didn't come here just to find out what I thought of the horse, did you?" Fontaine said. "Perhaps you thought I had a man watching you?"

"That possibility had crossed my mind."

"I suppose that's not surprising, considering your reputation. But I can assure you, I have no interest in the Gunsmith. I'm a gambler, not a gunman."

"I understand you might have a few gunmen on your payroll."

"Now who could have told you that?" Fontaine wondered. "The sheriff perhaps?"

Clint didn't answer.

"Yes, well," Fontaine said, "I have men with all kinds of talents working for me. Could be some of them consider themselves to be gunmen. And if any of them are interested in you, that would be their business—and their problem, I suppose. I know I wouldn't want to go up against you with a gun, even if I could."

"You've got a man named Blacker working for you, don't you?"

"I do," Fontaine said, looking either genuinely surprised or feigning it. "What's your interest in Blacker?"

"I don't have any interest in him, really," Clint said. "I've just heard about him since I came to town."

"What have you heard?"

"That he might be one of those men you talked about to consider themselves a gunman."

"And you're afraid he might go after you?"

"Not afraid," Clint said, "but concerned."

"I can arrange an introduction, if you like," Fontaine said. "Then you could ask him yourself."

"That's not necessary," Clint said. "I think I got what I came here for."

"Really? I can't imagine I've said anything that would be important to you."

Clint stood up.

"I've taken up enough of your time."

As Clint turned to leave, Fontaine said, "Perhaps I could ask you some questions?"

Clint turned back.

"Sure."

"How do you think Whirlwind will do in the Derby?"

"I think he'll do well."

"Will he win?"

"I don't know," Clint said. "Unlike you, I don't have any information on the other horses."

"But you're a man who knows horseflesh," Fontaine said.

"You ran your gelding in tandem with the three-year-old. What did that tell you?"

"That the little horse is competitive," Clint said. "He'll try hard."

"I see. No predictions, eh?"

"I'd be guessing, not predicting, Mr. Fontaine," Clint said. "Thanks for seeing me. Have a good day."

"Same to you. Shall I have Gage show you out?"

"I'll find my own way out, thanks."

"Very well."

Clint left the room, got back to the front door without difficulty. Gage was waiting there, and opened the door for him.

"What's your name?" Clint asked.

"Gage, sir."

"Gage, do you bet on the horses?"

"Oh, no, sir," Gage said. "I work too hard for my money to gamble it. I leave that to Mr. Fontaine, and others."

"Probably a good idea," Clint said.

"Good day, sir," Gage said.

"Yes," Clint said, "good day to you, too."

Clint stepped outside, and Gage closed the door gently behind him. There were still no other men in sight, but Clint had the feeling he was being watched. As he mounted up and rode away, he felt an itch in the center of his back.

TWENTY-FOUR

Gage entered the office and looked at his boss, waiting for orders.

"Get me Blacker."

"Yes, sir."

Blacker walked into the office with none of Gage's subservient attitude. Rather, he walked with arrogance.

"Adams was just here," Fontaine said.

"I saw him."

"He asked me about you."

"Why would he do that?"

"Apparently somebody mentioned you."

"Nobody mentions me," Blacker said. "That's how I like it."

"Well, somebody did."

"Who?"

"I'm thinking maybe the sheriff."

"Hackett? Yeah, he's probably the only one. So what did you tell him?"

"About you? Nothing."

"Good. So whataya want me to do?"

"I don't know yet," Fontaine said. "I need time to think."

"There's only two more days 'til the Derby."

"I know that," Fontaine said. "Just stay around here 'til then. When I decide, I'll want to be able to get to you quick."

"Yeah, okay," Blacker said. "Okay. At least the grub around here ain't bad."

"Good idea," Fontaine said. "Go and get something to eat."

Blacker left and Fontaine poured himself a brandy. It was never too early for good brandy, and maybe it would help him think.

Clint got back to Louisville and reined in his horse in front of the sheriff's office. As he entered and found Hackett there, he wondered if the man ever left the building.

"Back already?" Hackett asked. "You talk to Fontaine?"

"I did. Didn't find out much. Claimed he never heard anything about Blacker being a gunman."

"He might be telling the truth."

"Yeah, he might be," Clint said. "But he did tell me something else."

"What's that?"

"That he also had somebody watching those other two out-of-town horses work out."

"So what do you want to do with that information?" Hackett asked.

"I thought I'd go and talk to those folks," Clint said. "Do you know where they're staying?"

"Well," Hackett said, "they each rented places out of town. One of them is at Two Chimneys, and the other—"

"Can you just give me directions? I want to talk to them."

"What do you hope to learn from them?"

"I don't know."

"So what questions will you ask?"

"I don't know that either," Clint said. "Not until I get there."

"Well, okay," Hackett said. "They're both only about an hour outside of town . . ."

Clint left the office armed with directions to both places, mounted up, and rode out again.

TWENTY-FIVE

Clint rode to Two Chimneys first, where Sunday Song was being stabled, and was working. According to Hackett, the horse's owner was William Kingston, and the trainer was Ollie Shoemaker.

As he rode up on the house and stable, nobody was in sight. It wasn't a working ranch, so that wasn't unusual. That was the way it had been at the Fontaine place, as well.

He stopped in front of the house, and as he did, a man came out of the barn and walked over.

"Help ya?" he asked.

"I'm looking for Kingston, or Shoemaker."

"I'm Shoemaker," the man said.

"The trainer?"

"That's right." Shoemaker gave Clint a suspicious look. "What's this about?"

"Well, I'm not really sure," Clint said. "My name is Clint Adams, and I'd like to talk to you and the owner, Mr. Kingston."

"You're Adams?" Shoemaker asked.

"That's right."

"I heard of you," the trainer said. "The Gunsmith, right?"

"That's right."

Shoemaker looked over at Eclipse.

"Impressive horse."

"Yes, he is."

"Ever think of racing him?"

"No."

"Too bad. He looks like he'd do really well in distance races."

"He does have a lot of stamina."

"Come into the house and I'll tell the boss you're here," Shoemaker said. "Can't guarantee he'll talk to you, though."

"That's fine."

They entered the house and Shoemaker said, "Wait here."

Clint nodded and waited, hat in hand. The entry hall of the house was very large, as was the house itself. Hackett had told him that the best training track in the county was here. Clint assumed it was behind the house, because he hadn't seen it.

Shoemaker returned and said, "Mr. Kingston is in the study."

"The study?"

"Yes, sir. Follow me."

Clint followed the tall, worn-looking trainer down a hall to a room which, like Fontaine's office, was lined with books, but it was much larger and had a lot more furniture than just a desk and chairs. Kingston and Shoemaker could have been the same age, mid-forties, but the owner looked like the healthier of the two and, also like Fontaine, was dressed impeccably.

"Mr. Adams?" Kingston asked.

"That's right."

"William Kingston." The man stuck out his hand, and

Clint shook it. "Ollie tells me you want to talk to us. What's it about?"

"Racing, I guess," Clint said.

"Well," Kingston said, "if you're looking for a tip on the Derby, I don't think I can help you."

"I've gotten nothing but tips on the Derby since I arrived," Clint said. "It's refreshing to find someone who doesn't have a tip."

Kingston laughed aloud and said, "Well, how about a drink?"

"Sure."

"Ollie?"

"Sure, boss."

"Brandy? Whiskey?" Kingston asked.

"I'll take a whiskey," Clint said.

"Me, too," Shoemaker said.

Kingston handed Clint a whiskey, and Shoemaker a shorter one. He poured a brandy for himself. There were a lot of plush chairs in the room, but they all remained standing.

"So, what's on your mind today, Mr. Adams?" Kingston asked.

"I think I should tell you first that Ben Canby is a good friend of mine."

"Canby?" Kingston said. "Doesn't he have a horse in the Derby?"

"We're not going to get anywhere if we dance around each other, sir," Clint said.

Kingston smiled.

"No, you're right," Kingston said. "Canby trains Whirlwind."

"Yes, he does."

"Are you here offering information, or looking for some?"

"I'm not sure," Clint said. "We've learned that a man named Peter Fontaine sent men out to watch Ben's horse, your horse, and the horse from the East as they worked out."

"I thought I noticed something in the distance," Kingston said. "Fontaine, you say. Isn't he a big man around these parts?"

"So I hear."

"So he's looking for an edge before he bets," Kingston said.

"Have you ever had any dealings with him?"

"I have not," Kingston said. "In fact, this is my first time east of the Mississippi. I do most of my business in California."

"Do you know the connections of the other horse? Uh, what is it? Easy Going."

"I have met the owner, Daniel Farnsworth," Kingston said. "But I haven't met the trainer, the Irishman, Seamus Callaghan."

"I have," Shoemaker said. "He's a good man. He'll have that horse ready."

"What are you thinking, Mr. Adams?"

"I just wonder if all Fontaine is up to is trying to make a winning bet," Clint explained. "It seems to me a man with his reputation would be after something much, much bigger."

"Like what?"

"That's the problem," Clint said with a shrug. "I don't know."

"Have you asked Mr. Fontaine?"

"I have," Clint said. "He wasn't very helpful."

"What about Dan Farnsworth?" Kingston asked. "Have you talked to him the way you're talking to me?"

"No," Clint said. "That was my next stop."

"Well," Kingston said, "I hope he's more helpful than I've been."

"So do I," Clint said. He set the glass down on a nearby table. "Thank you for the drink."

"You will let me know if you find out something I should be aware of, eh?"

"Definitely."

As Clint turned to leave, Kingston said, "Tell me something."

"What's that?"

"How good is that little horse, Whirlwind?"

"He'll give anybody a run for their money," Clint said.

"Ah," Kingston said, "good. Competition is very good."

"So I hear," Clint said.

He turned and left.

TWENTY-SIX

After Clint left, Shoemaker said, "What do you suppose that was about?"

"He's fishing."

"For what?"

"Answers."

"About what?"

"Ollie," Kingston said, "just train the horse, leave the rest of the thinking to me."

Shoemaker frowned.

Outside, Clint mounted up and started to ride out. As he passed the barn, a small black man stepped out, stopped short when he saw Eclipse.

"Wow," he said, "now that's a horse."

"Yes, it is."

"You racing him?"

"No, I'm afraid not. Besides, he's not three years old."

"I can see that."

"Are you riding Kingston's horse?"

"Sunday Song," the man said, "and I sure am."

"What's your name?"

"Lorenzo Capp," the man said.

"I hear Sunday Song is a good-looking horse himself," Clint said.

"He sure is. You wanna see him?"

"Can I?"

"Sure thing," Capp said. "Come on."

Clint dismounted and walked Eclipse into the barn.

Capp led Clint to a large stall with a locked door. Inside was a handsome three-year-old black colt. Clint had to admit that on looks alone, Sunday Song would beat Whirlwind.

"He's magnificent," Clint said.

"Yeah, he is."

"Is he fast?"

"The fastest," Lorenzo Capp said. "He's gonna win the Derby."

"Are you sure?"

"I've ridden a lot of horses, mister," Capp said. "This one is a winner. He ain't never been beat yet."

"I can't argue with credentials like that, can I?" Clint asked.

"No, sir," Capp said. "Are you friends with the boss?"

"I just left him," Clint said. "He's got a lot of faith in you, and this horse."

"He's a good boss," Capp said.

"And an honest man?" Clint asked.

"Like I said," Capp said, "he's a good boss."

"Well," Clint said, "I wish you luck, and I guess I'll see you on Derby day."

"Put your money on Sunday Song," Capp said. "He can't lose."

"I'll remember," Clint said.

TWENTY-SEVEN

Clint's next stop was the training facility of Easy Going. It was a smaller ranch than Two Chimneys, with no name posted over a wooden arch. Clint rode through the arch and up to the house, where a few men were milling about. The training track was right there in front. The men stopped to watch him as he dismounted. None of them approached him, but continued to watch.

He started up the steps to the house as the door opened and a man came out. He was sixty if he was a day, and the suit he wore led Clint to believe this was the owner of the horse, not the trainer. The man puffed on a pipe and watched as Clint ascended the steps.

"You don't look like a drummer," the man said, "and we're not selling anything, so what can I do for you?"

"Are you Mr. Farnsworth?" Clint asked.

"I am."

"My name is Clint Adams."

Farnsworth worked the stem of his pipe with his teeth as he thought a minute.

"I'm from New York," he said, "and this is my first time west, but that name means something to me."

"You might have heard it once or twice."

"Wait a minute," Farnsworth said, pointing at Clint with the pipe stem. "The Gunsmith, right? You were in New York some years ago with P. T. Barnum."

"I was."

"And then again with Buffalo Bill Cody."

"Yes."

"You're something of a legend out here."

"Well . . ."

"Sharpshooting, wasn't it?"

"Sometimes."

"Well, come in, sir, come in," Farnsworth said, opening the front door. "I'm very interested in what brings you here today."

Clint followed Farnsworth into the house. Smaller than the house at Two Chimneys, it was still well furnished but had no woman's touch to it. Not a home, Clint thought, just a place to stay.

"So what's this about?"

"The Kentucky Derby."

"Ah," Farnsworth said, "you want to know whether or not to make a bet on my horse? Well, I'll tell you, go to the bank, sir, go to the bank."

"No, that's not it."

"Then what is it?"

"Do you know a man named Peter Fontaine?"

Farnsworth took the pipe from his mouth and frowned at the wet stem.

"I know the name," he said. "He's a businessman with questionable methods. In fact, some say he's more of a gambler than a businessman."

"That's the man," Clint said.

"Are you here representing him?"

"Not at all," Clint said. "I'm a friend of Ben Canby's."

"Canby," Farnsworth said. "Another name I should know."

"He's a local trainer."

"Ah, yes," Farnsworth said. "Whirlwind, isn't it?"

"That's right."

"I've heard he's a nice little horse."

"He is that."

"Good," the man said. "My horse could use a little competition from somebody other than Sunday Song. But what's this all got to do with Fontaine?"

Clint explained that Fontaine had been having all three horses watched as they worked out.

"One day, maybe more," Clint said.

"How do you know this?"

"I tracked the watcher back to Fontaine's ranch. When I confronted him, he admitted it."

"And what does he say is the reason?"

"He'd like me to believe he was just looking for an edge in making a bet."

"But you don't believe it."

"No," Clint said. "A man like him must have another reason."

"Money."

"Yes."

"You think he's got some scheme cooked up to make money off this race, but it has more to do with simply placing a bet."

"Exactly."

"What were you hoping to get from me?" Farnsworth asked. "Confirmation?"

"No," Clint said, "I just wondered if you knew Fontaine, or had ever done business with him."

"As I said," Farnsworth said, "I've heard of the man, but no, I've never done business with him. Have you checked with Mr. Kingston?"

"I have," Clint said. "He doesn't know him either."

"That's odd."

"Why do you say that?"

"Well, he has his fingers in a lot of pies, does our Mr. Kingston. I would have thought he'd crossed swords with someone like Fontaine before."

"Maybe he lied to me."

"I wouldn't want to call anyone a liar," Farnsworth said. "I was just saying that it sounded strange."

"How is your horse doing, Mr. Farnsworth?"

Farnsworth frowned again.

"Is it you who is looking for an edge, Mr. Adams? Some inside information?"

"I was just inquiring about the health of your horse, sir."

"He's fine," the owner said. "My trainer is taking good care of him."

"Glad to hear it."

"I'm happy you're pleased."

"And thanks for talking to me."

"Not at all."

Farnsworth walked Clint to the door and out to the porch.

"If you happen to discover what Mr. Fontaine is up to, will you let me know?"

"Of course," Clint said.

"Then good luck to you."

Clint went down the steps and picked up Eclipse's grounded reins.

"That's quite a horse you have," Farnsworth said.

"Yes, he is."

"A Darley, isn't he?"

"Yes," Clint said.

"Do you mind if I ask how you came to own him?"

Clint mounted and said, "He was a gift from P. T. Barnum."

"I wish my trainer were here to see him."

"Maybe another time," Clint said. "I have to be going."

Farnsworth took the pipe from his mouth. "As I said, good luck."

"Thanks," Clint said.

Farnsworth remained on the porch until Clint was out of sight, then looked at his pipe—which had gone cold—and went back into the house to find a match.

TWENTY-EIGHT

Clint's options were to ride back to town, or back to Canby's house. If he rode to town, he'd miss out on Elena's cooking that night, but Louisville was actually closer, and on the way, so he decided to stop there.

Clint wanted to hear the word around town on the Derby. As he rode in, he noticed that the town had become more crowded, with only two days left before the big race. He tried a couple of saloons, but they were packed to the rafters. If he'd needed a hotel, he doubted that he'd be able to find a room. Lucky he was staying out at Canby's place. The restaurants—both the large ones and the small cafés—were also full. He hoped Elena would leave some food out for him to eat when he got back.

The talk around Louisville was mostly about the two horses coming in from out of town, Easy Going and Sunday Song. He heard about Whirlwind only among talk of other local horses, as well. Canby would be happy that his horse was being lumped in with the others, and was not anyone's standout.

Clint came out of a saloon where he'd been unable to find

a space at the bar, when surprisingly he ran into Sheriff Hackett.

"Well," Clint said, "you do leave your office."

"On occasion," Hackett said. "This town is busting with people now, so I've got to keep an eye out. I can't really trust my young deputies when things are this volatile."

"I don't blame you," Clint said. "I've seen a few fistfights already, having to do with the Derby."

"Everybody's got an opinion and is willing to fight for it."

"Does that include you?"

"I may have an opinion," the sheriff said, "but I'll keep it to myself, thanks. What are you up to?"

"I just came back from seeing those two out-of-town trainers," Clint said. "They're both pretty confident about their horses."

"Well, the early odds have them very close, almost co-favorites, in fact."

"Where are the odds posted?"

"Just outside the track. Have you been over there yet?"

"No, I haven't seen it."

"I think you'll be impressed with Churchill Downs."

"Who runs the track? And the Derby?"

"The Louisville Jockey Club."

"Do they have an office somewhere?"

"Yes, in an office near the track. You thinking of talkin' to them?"

"I am," Clint said, "but who do I talk to?"

"I would think the stewards."

"What are the stewards?"

"They're the ones who make the rules," Hackett said. "Decide who wins if the finish is close. What to do if somebody's cheating."

"Maybe they'd know something about Fontaine."

"I don't see why they would, unless he owns a horse."

That was something Clint had never considered, but now . . .

"What if he does?"

"What if who does what?" Hackett said. He was distracted by an altercation that was taking place across the street. Three cowboys seemed about to come to blows.

"Fontaine. What if he owns a horse and nobody knows it? Wouldn't this Jockey Club know?"

"You'd think," Hackett said. "I gotta go to work, Adams."

"Sure."

Hackett crossed the street to intervene before the three cowboys started fighting in the street.

Clint went in search of the Louisville Jockey Club.

TWENTY-NINE

Clint found the Louisville Jockey Club housed in a new two-story brick building, on the second floor. He had to talk to a hatchet-faced, middle-aged secretary before he got in to see a man named Justin Stein, who was the head steward.

The man greeted Clint at his door with his hand out. He was tall, gray-haired, in his fifties.

"A pleasure, Mr. Adams," he said. "I know your reputation. Are you here for the Derby?"

"The Derby is what brought me to Louisville, yes," Clint said. "My friend Ben Canby has a horse entered."

"Oh, yes," Stein said, "Mr. Canby has one of our local hopes. Whirlwind, isn't it?"

"That's right."

"Please, have a seat." The man circled his desk and sat. "Can I offer you something?"

"No, thank you," Clint said. "I'm really here to try and get some information."

"Really, Mr. Adams?" Stein asked. "Are you looking for a tip?"

"Not at all," Clint said. "I've had enough of those since I arrived."

"I'll bet," Stein said, then laughed at his own little joke.

"I'm interested in a man named Peter Fontaine."

"One of Louisville's leading citizens," Stein said. "What can I tell you about him?"

"How about, does he own any horses entered in the Derby?"

Stein frowned a moment.

"I'm not aware of Mr. Fontaine owning any race horses, let alone one entered in the Derby."

"Could he own a horse under a different name?"

"All owners must declare themselves to the Jockey Club," Stein said. "If anyone is found operating under an assumed name, they would be disqualified from the race, and stripped of their ownership."

"But it is possible, right?"

"I suppose anything is possible," Stein said. "But why all the questions?"

"Fontaine is up to something," Clint said. "I'm trying to figure out what."

"I don't see where I can help you, sir," Stein said. "This sounds like a matter for the law."

"He hasn't broken any laws," Clint said, "yet."

"Well," Stein said, "I suppose I could dig deeply into some of the horse ownerships."

"I'd appreciate that."

"But I don't know if I can do that until after the Derby."

"Well," Clint said, "maybe you could try."

"I'll see what I can do."

Clint extended his hand and said, "Thank you, sir." They shook hands and Clint left.

* * *

Outside, he wondered if he'd accomplished anything. Stein, as the head steward, probably had his hands full with preparations for the race. There was no way he'd have time to go deep into the ownership of the horses. Clint was just going to have to keep looking, or give up and go back to Canby's. Just stand by his friend while he ran his horse in the Kentucky Derby.

He was getting hungry, so he mounted up and rode out of Louisville.

"I've made a decision," Fontaine said.

"About time," Blacker said.

"Quiet," Gage said. "The boss is talking."

They were in Fontaine's office, with the door closed, even though the rest of the house was empty.

"Well," Blacker said, "what did you decide?"

"We can't move forward as long as Clint Adams is nosing around."

"No, sir," Gage said.

"Blacker," Fontaine said, "he has to be gotten rid of."

"Killed, you mean," Blacker said. "Say what you mean, Fontaine."

"Killed," Fontaine said, "Adams has to be killed."

"Okay, then," Blacker said. "I want double."

"What?"

"Double my usual fee," Blacker said.

"You're crazy."

"No," Blacker said, "I'm not crazy, that's the point. Do you know how many men have tried to kill the Gunsmith? And failed? This is not something new to him. It happens all the time."

"All right, all right," Fontaine said. "Double."

"Uh, sir?"

"Yes, Gage?"

"I want double, as well."

"Yes, all right," Fontaine said. "Double for you, too. But no one else, right? Don't tell anyone else."

"Don't worry," Blacker said. "Everyone else will work for wages."

"That's good," Fontaine said, "because there's a lot of money to be had here. I'm not looking to split it a dozen ways."

Blacker stood up, hitched up his holster.

"When do you want this done?"

"As soon as possible," Fontaine said. "We've got to move in two days."

"Do you have all the information you need?" Blacker asked.

"I thought the out-of-towners might have some security around them," the man said. "They don't. The only danger is Adams. At least, that's what you told me, right, Blacker?"

"You didn't send me to look at the other two," Blacker said. "I'm going by the information you gave me. As long as that information is good, then Adams is the only problem we have."

"It was your men who brought me that information," Fontaine said.

"Yeah, yeah," Blacker said. "Okay. I'll get the job done. You care how?"

"I don't want a Western shoot-out in the street," Fontaine said. "It would be better if Adams just disappeared."

"I can arrange that," Blacker said. "Since he seems to have got my name from somebody, I don't want him around here any more than you do."

"What about me?" Gage asked. "What am I to do?"

"Just sit tight," Blacker said. "I'll let you know."

He left.

"Boss?" Gage asked.

"Do what he says," Fontaine snapped. "Just sit tight."

THIRTY

Clint got back to Canby's, took Eclipse into the barn, and saw to his comfort before returning to the house. He peeked in on Whirlwind. The three-year-old stood still and stared back at him.

"What do you say, boy?" Clint asked him. "Should I put my money on you?"

The horse kept staring.

"That's what I thought," Clint said. "No tips when you're looking for one."

He left the barn and walked to the house. As he entered, he smelled the remnants of supper in the air. He went directly to the kitchen, found Elena there, cleaning the stove.

"Are you hungry?" she asked.

"I am," he said.

"I thought you might have eaten in Louisville."

"Too crowded."

"Not by half," she said. "Folks usually start pouring in the day before. Have a seat at the table. I'll bring something out."

"Thank you," Clint said. "Where's Ben?"

"In his room, I think."

"Asleep?"

"No," she said, "it's too early. He's probably reading."

"I'll wait at the table," Clint said, "rather than bothering him."

He went out to the dining room and sat down. Elena appeared after only a few minutes.

"I hope you don't mind cold chicken," she said. "I've cleaned the stove and oven already."

"Cold chicken is fine," he said.

"Actually, it's not so cold," she told him, setting the platter down.

He picked up a leg and felt what she meant. It hadn't gone fully cold yet.

"I'll bring some vegetables," she said. "They should be the same temperature."

"That'll be fine," Clint said.

He was on his second piece when she returned. She brought with her a pitcher of water.

"This okay?" she asked. "I can bring whiskey if you like."

"Water's fine."

"Do you mind if I sit with you while you eat?" she asked.

"No," he said, "I don't mind."

She sat across from him. He bit into the chicken. It was excellent, but by now he expected no less from the cook.

"What have you found out?" she asked.

"About what?"

"About whoever was watching."

Clint looked at her.

"How much has Ben told you?"

"Everything," she said. "He pretty much tells me everything."

He stopped chewing and stared.

"Don't be so shocked," she said.

"So you're more than just the cook?"

"Much more."

"Why does he—"

"He thinks he's protecting my reputation," she told him. "I've told him I don't care, but he won't hear of it. So . . . what have you found?"

While he ate, he told her everything he had learned, which really wasn't much.

"So you still don't know what Fontaine has planned," she said when he was done.

"No."

"All right then," she said. "I have something to tell you that might help."

He chewed a potato and asked, "What's that?"

"I think Peter Fontaine is a thief."

"Well," Clint said, "I'm sure a lot of his business associates probably agree."

"No," she said, "I mean he's really a thief. A bank robber. A train robber. A thief."

He stopped chewing, sat back, and wiped his mouth with a napkin.

"You're serious."

"Yes."

"Ben told me you used to work for Fontaine."

"For a short time," she said. "I left because I found out he's a thief."

"Okay," Clint said, "you keep saying that, but you still haven't told me how you know."

"Well, keep eating," she said. "Do you have enough there?"

"I have plenty of food, Elena," he said. "What I don't have is enough information."

"Well," she repeated, "keep eating and I'll tell you."

THIRTY-ONE

"I cooked for Mr. Fontaine for five months," she said. "During that time he had all kinds of men in and out of his house. Some of them were businessmen. But some of them were . . . not businessmen."

"What were they?"

"I believe they were gunmen."

"Do you know any names?"

"Well . . . Mr. Gage—"

"His butler? Or houseman? Whatever he is?"

"Mr. Gage is no one's butler," she said. "He's very good with a gun."

"Is that a fact?"

"Well, he was when he was younger," she said.

"How do you know this?"

"People often talk around a cook like she isn't there," she explained.

Clint couldn't argue with that. He'd done it a time or two himself.

"There was also a Mr. Blacker."

"Now that name I've heard."

"He's in charge of the men Mr. Fontaine employs who are not businessmen. Gunmen."

"And what does Mr. Fontaine have these gunmen do?"

"I told you," she said. "Rob banks and trains, payrolls, things like that."

"Does Mr. Fontaine himself ever go out and do these things?"

"No," she said, "he plans them."

"And how do you know that?"

"I brought him something to eat one day in his office," she said. "When I returned to pick up the tray, he wasn't there, but he had left some . . . paperwork on the desk."

"Paperwork?"

"Plans," she said, "which seemed to be for a bank in Saint Louis."

"Why didn't you tell the sheriff?"

She bit her lip.

"I wasn't sure," she said. "I mean, maybe I misinterpreted what I saw. But I did stop working for Mr. Fontaine. I just wasn't comfortable staying there."

Clint chewed as he thought.

"So Fontaine is a planner."

"Is that what they call it?" she asked.

"I've run across men over the years who are very smart. They plan jobs, and then send other men out to put their plan into action."

"So I was right?"

"Probably. You seem like a smart lady. I don't see you as someone who jumps to conclusions, or misinterprets what she sees."

"Thank you."

"No," Clint said, "thank you. Now we know Fontaine is planning something."

"Like what?"

"Something that made it necessary for him to keep tabs on Easy Going, Sunday Song . . . and me."

"But why?"

"Maybe because we're all from out of town."

"And why would that be important?"

"Because he knew what he was dealing with when it came to people who lived here," Clint said, "but we were unknowns to him."

"And now?"

"He's found out who I am," Clint said. "That may pose a problem for him if he's planning a job."

"But why?" she asked again. "If the jobs he plans are out of town, why would it bother him that you're in Louisville?"

Clint stopped eating.

"What is it?" she asked.

"What if," Clint said, "the job he's planning is not out of town, but right here in Louisville?"

"What kind of job would that be?"

"I don't know," Clint said, "a local bank maybe?"

"Why would he suddenly decide to pull a job where he lives?" she asked.

"Maybe he's moving," Clint said. "Maybe it's such a big job that it's worth the risk. Maybe—"

"Maybe," Ben Canby said from the door, "it's the Derby."

Clint and Elena both turned their heads to look at Canby.

"What?" Clint asked.

"There are going to be a ton of people at the track," Canby said. "They will have paid admission, and wagered a fortune on the race."

Clint thought a moment, then said, "Jesus. He's going to rob the Kentucky Derby."

THIRTY-TWO

"You're crazy," Sheriff Hackett said.

It was the next morning and Clint was sitting in the sheriff's office. He had just told Hackett his theory—the theory he'd formed with both Elena and Ben Canby.

"Think about it."

"First of all," Hackett said, "Elena Willis didn't quit her job with Fontaine, she was fired. Don't you think she might be just trying to make some trouble for him?"

"How do you know that?"

"At the time. Fontaine claimed she had stolen something from him," Hackett said. "I looked into it, and couldn't prove anything either way. I got Fontaine to drop the charges, though."

"That was nice of you."

"I was just doing my job."

"But it's still just Fontaine's word against hers," Clint said.

"I know that, but . . . to accuse him of planning robberies? That's ridiculous."

"Why?"

"Because he's a businessman."

"Are you sure?"

"What?"

"Have you ever checked to see if he's really a businessman?"

"Well . . . no."

"Maybe you should."

"Based on what?" Hackett asked. "Your suspicions?"

"The Derby is tomorrow," Clint said. "Do you really want to take a chance?"

Hackett opened his mouth to answer, then closed it and thought a moment.

"Okay," he said, "I'll look into it."

"While you're at it," Clint said, "you might want to check on Churchill Downs' security."

"I know my job, Adams."

"Yes, all right," Clint said. "I'm sure you do."

"So get lost and let me do it."

"Right," Clint said. "Okay."

He turned and left the office, hoping that the sheriff was serious, and wasn't just trying to humor him.

After Clint Adams left his office, the sheriff went looking for one of his deputies. He was going to need somebody to watch the office for a while.

Fontaine looked at Sheriff Hackett as Gage let him into the house, led him into the living room.

"You're not supposed to come here," he said. "What if somebody saw you?"

"Nobody did," Hackett said.

"This better be important."

"It is," Hackett said. "The Gunsmith came to see me."

"About what?"

"You," Hackett said. "He's figured it out, Fontaine."

"Has he?"

"He knows you're gonna hit the Derby."

Fontaine firmed his jaw.

"What did you say?"

"That I'd look into it," Hackett said. "You've got to take care of him, Pete. I don't want him coming after me."

"He won't," Fontaine said.

"Are you sure?"

"It's already being handled," Fontaine said, "as we speak. You just get back to town and be ready to do your job."

"All right," Hackett said, "if you say so."

Gage showed the lawman out, then came back.

"He's gonna fold," Gage said.

"Don't worry," Fontaine said, "the unfortunate sheriff is gonna catch a bullet during the robbery. He's gonna die a hero."

"And Adams?"

"He's just gonna die."

THIRTY-THREE

Clint went to the nearest saloon for a beer. It turned out to be the saloon where Jesse worked. He'd forgotten that.

"Hey, stranger," she said, coming up next to him.

It was early, the place was mostly empty, and she wasn't dressed for work. Instead of a brightly colored gown, she wore a simple blue cotton dress.

"Hello," he said, turning to her while holding his beer.

"What have you been doing?" she asked. "Haven't seen you in here since last time."

"I've been keeping busy," he told her.

"Too busy to come and see me?"

"I'm sorry."

"Busy like everybody else?" she asked. "Trying to figure out which horse to bet on?"

"No," Clint said, "I know which horse to bet on."

"How did you figure that out?"

"Like you said," he answered. "Disregard all the tips, bet what's left."

"Smart man." She put her hand on his arm. "I'm not busy now. You wanna come upstairs?"

"Men usually have to pay to go upstairs, don't they?" he asked.

"Like I said," she replied, rubbing his arm, "I'm not workin'."

He studied her for a moment, then said, "All right."

"Bring the beer," she said, taking his free hand.

He took a chance, carrying the beer in his right hand while she led him by the left. He wondered if he'd get up the stairs, but before long they were there, walking to her door. She opened it, and drew him inside, closing the door behind her.

She moved away from him, then turned and smiled. She peeled the dress down from her shoulders, exposing herself little by little.

He watched, sipping the beer as the dress pooled at her feet and she kicked it away. She wore no undergarments, and was gloriously naked. She smiled again, cupped her breasts in her hands, used her thumbs to flick the nipples until they were distended.

He knew his attention was supposed to be fixed on her, but he could hear the footsteps in the hallway behind him.

As she spread her legs and reached down between them, probing herself with her fingers, the door suddenly slammed open. She had closed but not locked it.

He dropped the beer mug and turned. Before it shattered on the floor, his gun was out and he was firing.

There were three men in the hall, two framed in the doorway and one behind them. Their guns were out, but they had no chance. The two in the door folded over as his slugs struck them in the belly, their guns falling from their hands. They got a few shots off, but they went wild.

The third man started running down the hall. Clint stepped over the dead men and raced after him.

"Stop!" he shouted at the fleeing man.

He wanted to talk to him, but the man turned with his gun in his hand.

Clint let the man get off a shot, but in the end he had no choice. He fired, striking the man in the chest and the belly. He fell to the floor, dead.

Clint moved down the hall and checked the body, then returned to the room to check the other two. When he looked at Jesse, he saw her lying on the ground, bleeding from a bullet wound in her chest, right between her breasts.

THIRTY-FOUR

Clint was waiting in the saloon when Sheriff Hackett arrived.

"What happened?" he demanded.

"You don't know?"

"I just got here, Adams."

"You got some dead men upstairs," Clint said. "And a dead woman."

"Woman?"

"Jesse," the bartender said.

"You know what happened?" the lawman asked the barkeep.

"Three men went after him when he went upstairs with Jesse," the bartender said. "That's all I know."

Hackett looked up toward the second floor, then back at Clint.

"Don't go away."

"I'm not going anywhere."

Hackett nodded, went upstairs to have a look.

"Let me have another beer," Clint said to the bartender. "I spilled the other one."

* * *

Clint was working on the beer when the sheriff came down.
At the same moment his two deputies came through the
batwings. Clint saw them in the mirror.

The sheriff walked up to him.

"You killed three men and a woman, Adams," Hackett
said. "I'll need your gun."

"I killed three men," Clint said. "They killed the woman.
And I'm not giving you my gun, Sheriff."

"You defying the law, Adams?"

"I'm defying you," Clint said.

"Why do you want to do this the hard way?"

"There isn't any other way to do it," Clint said. "You're
in Fontaine's pocket. Did you think I didn't know that?"

Hackett wet his lips.

"Don't risk your young deputies on this move, Hackett,"
Clint said. "Go back to Fontaine, tell him this didn't work,
and you tried to do your job."

Hackett wet his lips again.

"Sheriff?" one of the deputies said.

"Stand down," Hackett said.

"But—" the other started.

"I said stand down!"

The two deputies relaxed.

"Get out!" Hackett said. "Go back to the office."

The two young men backed their way to the door, then
went out.

Hackett looked around. There were a few men in the
saloon, watching the action. Then he looked at the
bartender.

"Give me a beer."

The bartender did.

"You should leave town," Hackett said.

"Who else is in on this, Sheriff?"

"Why risk your life for somebody else's money?" the lawman asked.

"I'm not leaving, Sheriff," Clint said. "Tell Fontaine that. Tell him next time to send somebody better. Are any of those men up there Blacker?"

"No."

"Then tell him to send his best."

"I ain't said I work for him," Hackett reminded Clint.

"You don't have to," Clint said. He finished his beer, put his mug down. "Don't be around when they come after me again, Sheriff."

"You'd shoot a lawman?" Hackett said.

"No," Clint said, "but I'd shoot you."

Outside, Clint tensed, waited for another attack, but apparently it wasn't coming. Somebody had expected the three men to get the job done, and had not set up a backup plan.

Somebody was going to be very disappointed.

"What's going on, Sheriff?" the bartender asked.

"Never mind."

"What's he talkin' about, you workin' for Fontaine?" the man asked.

"Shut up!" Hackett said. "It's none of your business."

"Okay, then," the bartender said, "what about the bodies upstairs?"

"I'll have them removed."

Hackett drained his beer, slammed the mug down, and then went out the batwings. He didn't see Adams anywhere, and stepped into the street. He didn't relish going back to Fontaine and telling him what had happened.

THIRTY-FIVE

"They did what?" Canby asked.

"Tried to kill me," Clint said.

"Are you all right?" Elena asked.

"I'm fine," Clint said.

They were in the living room of Ben Canby's house.

"What happened exactly?" Canby asked.

"They sent three guns against me."

"You killed them?" Elena asked.

"I did."

"Anyone else hurt?" Canby asked.

"A saloon girl," Clint said. "She's dead."

"The poor girl," Elena said.

"Don't feel too bad for her," Clint said. "She lured me in there to get me killed."

"I'll get some coffee," Elena said, and left the room.

"Sorry to shock her," Clint said.

"Don't worry about it," Canby said. "Believe me, she's not shocked. Neither am I. What'd the sheriff say about it?"

"The sheriff," Clint said, "is in Fontaine's pocket."

"No."

"Yes."

"Hackett?" Canby said, shocked. "I thought he was a decent man."

"But a bad checker player. Yes, I know."

"Do you think I was lying?" Canby asked.

"No, no," Clint said, "nothing like that."

"So what do we do for law?" Canby asked. "Who's gonna stop them from robbing the Derby tomorrow?"

"Well," Clint said, "I guess I am."

"You are what?" Elena asked, coming in with a tray.

"Clint says the law is in Fontaine's pocket," Canby said, "so he's gonna stop them from robbing Churchill Downs tomorrow."

"How do you propose to do that?" she asked, pouring coffee for them.

"He's bound to have a gang hitting the track," Canby said. "How are you gonna go up against that many men? Alone?"

"I may have to figure out a way to do something," Clint said, "before the Derby."

"All three?" Fontaine asked.

"And the girl," Hackett said.

"And you didn't arrest him?"

"I . . . wasn't gonna go up against him with two green deputies," Hackett said. "That's Blacker's job, not mine. Where is he?"

"He's out there," Fontaine said. "Don't worry, he's got a plan."

"Are you sure?"

"I'm sure," Fontaine said. "Adams has to be dead before the race tomorrow."

"Your men are gonna hit the track during the Derby?" Hackett asked.

"Don't you worry about that," Fontaine said. "You just do your part."

"I'll do my part," Hackett said. "As long as I get paid."

"You'll get paid," Fontaine said. "Everybody's going to get paid." Fontaine looked at Gage, who was standing in the door of the office. "Everybody is going to get what they deserve."

Elena had gone to the kitchen while Clint and Canby drank coffee and discussed the situation.

"What about killin' him?" Canby asked.

"Killing who?"

"Fontaine."

"Who's going to kill him? You?"

"No," Canby said. "I mean you."

"You want me to just walk in and kill him?" Clint asked.

"Dumb idea, huh?"

"I don't just kill people for no reason," Clint said. "They usually have guns in their hands."

"Well, what then?"

"I suppose," Clint said, "I could go and see him, and tell him I know what he's planning."

"But you don't."

"Not his exact plan," Clint said. "But I know what he's basically planning on doing. I could also go to the Jockey Club and tell them to beef up their security."

"You think they would? Based on your word?"

"Probably not," Clint said. "They'd probably want to check with the sheriff."

"And we're back to that again," Canby said. "Maybe I should just pull my horse. I mean, what's the point of running if there's not going to be any money?"

"What about actually having the Kentucky Derby winner?"

"That would be nice," Canby said, "but I'd also like the purse money."

"Okay, then," Clint said, putting his coffee cup down and standing, "then let's make sure you do."

THIRTY-SIX

There was no time for Clint to send for any help. And Canby was no hand with a gun. There was only one person Clint thought he could go to for help.

He found John Sun Horse in the fourth saloon he looked in. It was coming on midday and the small saloon was filling up. Sun Horse had a table in the back. Clint approached the table without bringing a beer with him this time.

"Sun Horse."

The Cherokee looked up from the beer mug he'd been staring into.

"Your hands are empty."

"Yes, they are," Clint said. He sat across from the Cherokee. "I need your help."

"I do not usually talk without a fresh beer," the Indian reminded him.

"I don't have the time to sober you up, John," Clint said.

"What is it?"

"I found out what Fontaine is up to," Clint said, and went on to explain . . .

* * *

John Sun Horse pushed the remnants of his beer away when Clint finished his story.

"What do you want me to do?" he asked. "I am a tracker."

"You must know some men who know how to use guns," Clint said.

"Perhaps."

"I need them."

"To do what?"

"To protect the track."

"Do they not have security for that?"

"I'm going to talk to the security people and offer them our help," Clint said. "But I have to know that I have help to offer."

"The race is tomorrow."

"I know."

"You have not given me much time to come up with a fighting force."

"But can you do it?"

"Will I be paid?"

"Yes."

"Will they be paid?"

"I'm sure I can get the track to pay a reward once we save their money." He wasn't sure, at all.

"How many men will you need?"

"I don't know," Clint said. "How many can you get?"

"On short notice? I do not know."

"Will you try?"

The Cherokee nodded.

"I will try," the Indian said. "Meet me back here in two hours."

"Good," Clint said. "I'm going to the track now. Thank you, Sun Horse."

"Do not thank me yet."

* * *

Clint went to Churchill Downs and paid his admission to get in. There were races going on, but he wasn't interested in that. He found a security guard.

"Where's your boss?"

"In his office, I guess," the bored guard said.

"Where is that?"

The man pointed and gave Clint directions.

"Thanks. By the way, what's his name?"

"Butler," the guard said, "Captain Sam Butler."

Clint followed the directions, found a door marked SECURITY, and knocked.

"Come!" a deep voice called out.

He opened the door and walked in. A barrel-chested man with thick arms and an even thicker mustache eyed him from behind a desk. He wore a uniform with a badge on his chest. Clint had the feeling he was looking at an ex-lawman.

"What do you want?" the man asked. "Who are you?"

"Captain Butler?"

"That's me."

"My name is Clint Adams."

The man eyed Clint and asked, "On the level?"

"On the level."

"I heard you were in town." Butler stood and extended his hand. Clint shook it. "What can I do for you?"

"I think the question is, what can I do for you?" Clint said.

"What do you mean?" Butler asked. "What could you do for me?"

"Maybe save your job," Clint said, "and save the track a lot of money."

Butler sat back down.

"I'm listening."

THIRTY-SEVEN

Captain Butler listened to what Clint had to say, sitting stock-still the whole time. When Clint finished, the man shook his head.

"Can't be done."

"What do you mean?"

"Our security is too good," Butler said. "There's no way anybody can rob us."

Clint had heard that before from the securest of banks.

"Anyone's security can be beat, Captain."

The man firmed his jaw and said, "Not mine."

"I have information that indicates you're going to be hit," Clint reminded him. "Why don't you show me your security so I can—"

"If you'll excuse me, Mr. Adams," Butler said. "I know your reputation, and there's nothing in it that says you're a security expert."

"I'm not trying to—"

"I thank you for bringing this to my attention," Butler said, "but if someone is going to try to hit us, I welcome the attempt. They'll have a big surprise coming to them. Good day."

Clint sat there for a moment, but he recognized that the man had shut down and would not be listening to anything else he had to say on the subject.

He stood up and left without another word.

Clint made a circuit of the track, trying to figure out what Captain Butler was so proud of. There were guards everywhere, including the area where the bets were made. For the most part, though, Clint thought they looked as bored as the first guard he'd encountered.

There could only be two reasons Butler was so sure his security couldn't be breached. First, it was so good that Clint couldn't figure it out, or second . . . like the sheriff, he was also in the pocket of Peter Fontaine.

That had to be it. Fontaine had managed to buy both the local law and the heads of security at the track. The take of this robbery was probably so huge he could afford to buy everybody he needed. In the end, he probably didn't intend to actually pay any of them, but they were too greedy to realize it.

He was going to have to do this himself, with whatever assistance he could get from John Sun Horse.

Clint headed back to the saloon. When he walked in, he saw the bartender, John Sun Horse, and five more Indians. Other than that, the saloon was empty.

Clint approached the bartender.

"What's going on?" Clint asked.

"You tell me," the bartender said. "Sun Horse walked in here with five of his friends, and the rest of my customers left."

"Oh, well, that might be my fault. I asked Sun Horse to meet me here with his friends."

"Well then, could you get them out of here?"

"I could, yes I could," Clint said, "but first I have to have a meeting with them. So could you please give each of them a drink? One drink."

"I ain't servin' no Indian any whiskey," the man said.

"Okay then, bring them each a beer, please, at that back table. And one for me. That's seven beers."

"Well, only because I ain't got anybody else in here buyin' drinks."

"Fine," Clint said, "whatever the reason is, bring them over to that table."

Clint left the bar and walked over to where Sun Horse was sitting with his friends.

"Sun Horse," Clint said.

"Mr. Gunsmith."

"So . . . these are your men?"

"These are the men you asked me to find," Sun Horse said.

Clint looked at the five Cherokee. Two of them were sixty if they were day, only it was hard to tell with Cherokee. They could have been eighty. The others were certainly over fifty.

"Each of these men can handle a gun," Sun Horse said.

Clint looked at the men and said, "I don't see any guns."

"Oh, I did not say they owned guns, I said they can handle one," Sun Horse said. "You will have to buy them guns. And I mean rifles. They cannot handle revolvers."

"Well . . . all right," Clint said as the bartender came over with the beers. The eyes of each Cherokee lit up and they made a grab for a mug each.

"Hold on now," Clint said, "before you drink any of that."

They all stopped, including Sun Horse.

"I'll buy a rifle for each of you," Clint said, "and tell you what to do, but you have to agree that until you're finished working for me, this will be the last drink you have."

They all looked at Sun Horse.

"And after?" he asked Clint.

"I'll buy each man a bottle of whiskey."

"And the rifles?" Sun Horse asked.

"You will be able to keep the rifles."

Sun Horse looked at the five Cherokee and spoke to them in their own language.

"They don't understand English?" he asked.

"They do," Sun Horse assured him. "They will understand your orders. I just wanted to make sure they understood everything before they all agreed."

"And?"

Sun Horse raised his mug and said, "We will all be working for you, Mr. Gunsmith."

"Mr. Gunsmith," his friends echoed.

Clint picked up his beer and said, "All right, then. Drink your beer and I'll tell you what you're supposed to do."

THIRTY-EIGHT

"So what we have to do," Sun Horse said later, "is keep the racetrack from being robbed tomorrow?"

"Yes."

"That does not seem to be so hard."

"Now," Clint said, "I warn you, I don't know how many men will be involved."

"White men?" Sun Horse asked.

"Most likely."

"Then it does not matter," the Indian said. "One Cherokee is worth any five white men."

"Sun Horse," Clint said. He took the man's arm and drew him away from the others, who were still working on their beers. "How old are these men?"

"That does not matter," Sun Horse said. "They can all shoot."

"That may be, but—"

"Did I not do the job you asked me to do?" Sun Horse asked. "Find and track the man you were after. Ride with you, keep up with you?"

"Well, yeah, you did."

"Do you know how old I am?"

"Well . . ." Clint said. He studied Sun Horse for a few moments. The man's face was weathered from constant exposure to the sun over the years. So he added ten years to his guess. "Sixty?"

"I'm seventy-two," Sun Horse said. "I'm older than all of these men. Do not worry. They will be able to do the job."

"Well," Clint said, "all right." He turned to the other men. "Finish up those beers. We've got to go and get you your rifles."

All five men nodded and upended their beer mugs.

When they came out of the gunsmith's shop, all six Cherokee were carrying Winchesters.

"Now what?" Sun Horse asked.

"Now," Clint said, "let's find someplace for them to try out their rifles. Once they're all comfortable, we'll go over to the track."

"There's an empty lot two blocks over," Sun Horse said.

"Lead the way, Sun Horse."

In the empty lot, which was behind the feed and grain building, Clint watched while the Cherokee tried out their rifles. He was impressed by the ability of each man to hit what he shot at—especially Sun Horse.

"Well?" Sun Horse asked.

"I'm satisfied," Clint said. "Line them up so I can talk to them."

Sun Horse got them in a straight line, holding their rifles.

"We're going over to the track to see how many entrances they have," he said. "I'm going to post one man at each entrance—or as many entrances as we can cover."

"How will we know who to let in and who to stop?" Sun Horse asked.

"I'll want you to stop anyone from entering around the time of the race," Clint said.

"Will some of them not get in before that?" Sun Horse asked.

"You and I will be inside, Sun Horse," Clint said. "We'll take care of any of them who get in."

"Whatever you say, Mr. Gunsmith," Sun Horse said. "You are the boss."

"Come on, then," Clint said. "Let's find each man his post."

THIRTY-NINE

Clint found he was able to cover all of the public entrances with the Cherokee at his disposal. There were others that were available to owners, trainers, and jockeys, as well as employees of the track, but he felt the robbers would probably get in through the public entries.

"All right," he said, "now we know where to be tomorrow."

They all nodded.

"Sun Horse," he said, "I expect you to keep them sober 'til then."

"They do not drink when they are working," Sun Horse said. "Just like me."

"Okay, then," Clint said. "I'll meet you all right out here. Let's make it the beginning of the racing day."

"As you say," Sun Horse said. "What will you be doing until then?"

"There's somebody I want to see," Clint answered. "I'm thinking I might be able to cut this off at the source. If not, I'll see you all here tomorrow."

Sun Horse nodded, and they went their separate ways.

Clint hoped the others were as trustworthy as John Sun
Horse.

Clint rode out to Fontaine's place. If he could convince the
man to call the robbery off, it might save a lot of trouble,
and lives.

He reined in Eclipse in front of the house and dismounted. No one was around as he mounted the steps to the
door. He started to knock when he saw that the door was
ajar. He pushed it open and entered.

"Hello?"

No answer.

"Anyone here?"

Still no answer.

Was the house deserted?

He went to Fontaine's office, found it empty. Then he
searched the second floor. And found nothing.

Fontaine was gone.

But the question was, had he gone willingly? Perhaps
into hiding until the robbery was over? Or had he been
taken? And if so, by whom? And for what purpose?

Clint took another walk through the house. There was no
signs of a struggle, no blood. Fontaine and Gage were both
gone, but the closets in the bedrooms were still full of clothes.

He turned and went out the front door.

Fontaine opened the door of the small house and went
inside.

"I haven't been here in many years," he said. "Smells
musty."

"I'll air it out," Gage said. "How long will we have to
stay here?"

"Just a few days," Fontaine said. "There are supplies in
the root cellar."

"I'll take a look, see how much there is," Gage said.

Fontaine nodded. This was where they would live until the job was done, and for some time after. Adams wouldn't be able to find him here. Of course, that was if Adams managed to avoid being killed by Blacker—which he hoped would not be the case.

Gage went around the small house, opening the windows and the shutters. The inside of the house immediately felt better, less stuffy.

"How will we know for sure when it's over?" Gage asked.

"Blacker knows where we are," Fontaine said. "He'll tell us."

Gage turned and faced his boss. He'd been working for Fontaine for many years, since they were both younger men. He had an almost fatherly concern for the man, as well as a paternal pride.

"What if he doesn't?" Gage asked. "What if he has other ideas?"

"You mean, what if Blacker double-crosses us?" Fontaine asked.

"Yes."

The younger man seemed to give that some thought before answering.

"Well," Fontaine said, "I guess we'll just have to trust him."

"Who are you kidding, Peter?" Gage asked with a snort of derision. "You don't trust anybody."

"That's not true, Gage," Fontaine said. "I trust you."

The older man gave him a long look.

"Well," Fontaine said, "I trust you as much as I trust anyone."

FORTY

Clint returned to Ben Canby's place, walked Eclipse into the barn, where he found the groom, Frank Dunlap.

"I'll take him, Mr. Adams."

"How's Whirlwind?"

"I'm getting him ready to travel to the track," Frank said.

"What about Alicia?"

"Ain't seen her for a while."

"Okay," Clint said, handing Eclipse's reins to Frank. "Thanks."

He walked to the house, found Canby sitting in the living room, going over some papers. He looked up when Clint entered, removed the wire-framed glasses he was wearing. Clint could smell supper cooking.

"What's going on?" Canby asked.

Clint sat down in a chair and described his day to his friend.

"You're takin' it on yourself to stop this robbery?" Canby said. "Why not call in federal help?"

"It would take them too long to get here," Clint said.

"So you're gonna use six Cherokee Indians to prevent a robbery?"

"I'm going to try."

"What about me?"

"What about you?"

"Should I take Whirlwind to the race?"

"The race is going to happen," Clint said. "If you want to win it, I suggest you be there."

"Well, okay, then," Canby said.

"Supper's ready!" Elena called to them from the dining room.

"Let's eat," Canby said, "and then I can check on Whirlwind."

"Frank said he's getting him ready to travel," Clint said as they walked to the table.

"Is he? Then he's more sure than I am that we're gonna run."

Elena brought a platter of steaks out and said, "Everybody's more sure about it than you are," then went back to the kitchen.

"Quiet, woman!" Canby called as she went back to the kitchen.

Her laughter came back to them from behind the closed door.

After supper they both went out to the barn to watch Frank with Whirlwind.

"Where's Alicia?" Clint asked.

"Haven't seen her."

"Is she gone?"

"I don't think so. She still lives here, as far as I know."

Frank inspected the three-year-old's legs.

"What about Fontaine?" Canby asked. "Where do you think he is?"

"I've decided he's gone into hiding."

"From you?"

"I suppose."

"Until after the job?"

"Probably," Clint said. "Or until Blacker can kill me."

"You think he's gonna try before tomorrow?" Canby said.

"Before the race," Clint said.

"And who's gonna watch your back?"

"John Sun Horse."

"Sun Horse? Can you trust him?"

"I have to," Clint said. "I mean, I'd prefer somebody I know better, but from what I've seen, he's competent."

"Listen," Canby said, "I can use a gun. How about if I—"

"You've got a job, Ben," Clint said. "Get this horse to the starting line. Leave the rest to me, okay?"

"Are you gonna have time to make a bet?"

Clint slapped his friend on the back and said, "I'll make time."

Outside, as darkness fell, Blacker moved through it. He found a place to hide. From there he could see both the house and the barn. He knew Clint and Canby were inside the barn. All he needed was one clean shot at Adams to get him out of the way. He took his gun out, checked his loads, and then holstered it again.

He was ready.

All he needed now was for the Gunsmith to come out of the barn.

FORTY-ONE

"I'll go back to the house," Clint said, "let you work with your horse."

"I'll be along soon," Canby said.

"If I don't see you, I'll be getting an early start tomorrow morning," Clint told him. "I've got to get to that track early."

"So will we," Canby said. "We'll ride together."

"That suits me," Clint said.

He walked to the door of the barn, then stopped.

"What is it?" Canby asked.

"Listen."

Canby came up next to him, and they both stood there listening.

"I don't hear anything."

"I know," Clint said. "No crickets, or birds. Nothing."

"Yeah," Canby said. "That's odd."

"Something's out there," Clint said.

"Wolf?" Canby asked. "Big cat?"

"Something," Clint said, "or somebody."

"What are you gonna do?"

"I'm going out the back," Clint said. "You stay in here, keep an eye on your horse."

"You think somebody's after Whirlwind?" Canby asked.

"Him," Clint said, "or me."

Blacker kept his eyes glued to the front of the barn. They must have been in there getting the horse ready for travel. Adams had to come out sometime. He wasn't doing anybody any good in there. Canby and his groom could handle the horse.

Where was he?

Clint went out the back door of the barn, worked his way around to one side. There were some horses in the corral. If there was a wolf or a cat out there, they'd smell it. They were too calm. To him, that meant only one thing.

There was a man out there, in the dark.

Waiting.

He looked around for a likely place for a man to hide. There were a few, but only hiding in the copse of trees beyond the corral would silence the insects.

He moved back to the rear of the barn, then worked his way around the corral until he was behind those trees. Despite a bright moon, it was too dark to read sign in the ground, but if there was a man in those trees, he would leave his horse farther down the trail.

Clint scouted a few hundred yards, almost quit when suddenly he heard something. Sounded like a horse nickering. He stood still, listened, heard it again, and followed it. He found a good-sized steeldust tied to a tree. He went through the saddlebags, found an extra shirt, a gun, bullets, and a letter sent care of General Delivery, Louisville. It was addressed to a man named Lucifer Blacker. No wonder he only went by his last name.

Now Clint had two choices. Wait for Blacker to get tired and come back to his horse, or go into those trees after him.

It all depended on the patience a man like Blacker had. Also, how determined he was to get rid of Clint before race day.

Clint decided to go in after him, just in case Blacker got itchy and shot the wrong man—such as Canby.

He headed back to the barn area.

"What do you think he's doing?" the groom, Frank, asked Canby.

"I don't know," Canby said. "It's still too quiet out there."

"Well, we're all done in here," Frank said. "When are we gonna leave?"

"Might be a man with a gun out there, Frank," Canby said. "If you want to go out, go on ahead."

Frank looked at the door nervously, then said, "Naw, I guess I'll wait."

"Good," Canby said, "then we'll just wait together."

Blacker saw some shadows just inside the door of the barn. It looked like two men, maybe getting ready to come out. He drew his gun, cradled it in both hands for a moment.

"Come on out, Gunsmith," he said to himself in low tones. "Come on out and get what's waiting for you."

"Maybe," Clint said from behind him, "you should step out of there and get what's coming to you, Mr. Blacker."

Blacker froze.

FORTY-TWO

"Adams?"

"The very one."

"You alone?"

"It's just you and me, Blacker," Clint said. "But don't think about spinning around and using that gun. I'd just as soon kill you as look at you. That's how I treat men who are waiting to bushwhack me."

"Now look," Blacker said, "let's talk about this. You have no idea how much money we're gonna get tomorrow."

"I think I have some idea."

"Well, there's always room to cut another man in," Blacker said. "Especially a man with your, uh, special talents."

"I don't think your boss Fontaine would agree with you," Clint said.

"I'm in charge of this operation," Blacker said.

"Well, that's too bad."

"Whataya mean?"

"What are your men going to do tomorrow when you don't show up?"

Blacker laughed low.

"They all know their jobs," Blacker said. "Whatever happens here, they'll pull that job tomorrow."

"You should have waited 'til tomorrow so you could be there with them."

"Well, Adams, to tell you the truth, I didn't wanna see you there, so I thought I'd get rid of you tonight."

"Seeing as how the other three men you sent—not to mention Jesse—didn't fare too well."

"You're right," Blacker said. "That's when I realized I'd have to do it myself. So whataya say you and me get outta these trees and face off, huh? Man to man?"

"Man to man?" Clint repeated.

"That's right."

"Who are you going to get to represent you?"

The one who grew impatient was Ben Canby.

"Okay," he said to Frank, "I'm headin' for the house. You with me?"

"Uh, I think I'll wait awhile longer."

"I'm thinkin' if anythin' was gonna happen, it woulda happened by now," Canby said.

"Boss . . ."

Canby stepped out and yelled, "Clint? You out there?"

Beyond Blacker, Clint could see the front of the barn. He saw Canby when he stepped out.

"Damn it!" Clint said.

Blacker was facing Canby with his gun already out. He had no chance.

"Ben! Down!" Clint yelled.

Blacker turned. He was fast, like a snake, and he almost got a shot off while Clint was yelling to Canby. But Clint was too fast. He fired once, and the bullet struck Blacker and spun him around so fast his gun went flying from his hand.

"Damn it!" Clint said again.

"Whataya mad at me for?" Canby asked later.

They were both standing, looking down at Blacker's body. Frank was standing farther behind them.

"You stepped out and I had to kill him," Clint said. "I wanted him alive."

"What for?"

"So he could tell me where Fontaine is."

"Well, if Fontaine's hiding, and Blacker's dead, doesn't that mean the robbery won't go off?"

"No," Clint said. "The plan is in play. According to Blacker, everybody knows their job. The robbery is going to happen. I just have to hope I have enough men to stop it."

"What about the Jockey Club?" Canby asked. "Maybe we can convince them together to increase the security."

"It's too late," Clint said. "The gates are going to open tomorrow and I have to be there."

"And so do I."

"All right," Clint said. "We'd better turn in, then."

"What about him?"

"What about him?" Clint echoed.

"What are we gonna do with him?"

"Leave him there for now," Clint said. "Cover him up. In the morning you can have somebody take him to town."

"And do what?"

"Dump him in the sheriff's lap," Clint said. "Maybe that'll shake him up some."

Canby told Frank to get a blanket out of the barn and put it over the body, then started back to the house with Clint.

"Tomorrow's gonna be one helluva day," he said.

He got no argument.

FORTY-THREE

In the morning they loaded Whirlwind onto a carrier and set out for Louisville, Churchill Downs, and the Kentucky Derby.

Clint thought about riding into the track with Canby and the horse, but he had told Sun Horse and the others he'd meet them out front.

As the gate opened to admit Canby and the horse, Clint said, "I'll see you later."

"I hope so," Canby said. "And don't forget to get your bet in before you get killed."

"I'll make a note of it."

He rode around to the front of the track, where Sun Horse and the others were waiting. He didn't have time to put Eclipse in a livery, so he just dismounted and left him there. The horse wouldn't move, and he wouldn't let anybody move him.

"You ready?" Clint asked them.

"We are ready," Sun Horse said.

"Hey!"

Clint turned to see who had shouted. He saw a security guard coming his way.

"What are all these Indians doin' here?" the man demanded.

"Talk to your boss," Clint said.

"Huh?" the man asked dimly. He was about as smart as a donkey, Clint could see.

"Captain Butler?" Clint said. "He's your boss, right?"

"Right."

"Well, tell him you talked to Clint Adams," Clint said. "He'll know what it's about."

"Okay."

"Oh, one more thing," Clint said as the man started away.

"Yeah?"

"Tell him Blacker's dead, and Fontaine's missing."

"Huh?"

"Just tell him."

"I will," the man said. "I'll find out what's goin' on."

As the guard walked away, Clint said to the Cherokees, "Take your positions, and be ready."

Clint doubted the Cherokees would be able to pick out the robbers, but he knew that when trouble started, they would come running.

"Come on, Sun Horse."

They went to the front gate and paid their admission to get in. The crowd had already begun to file in. There would be seven races before the Derby, and people would continue to come in until then.

"Mr. Gunsmith?" Sun Horse said.

"Yeah?"

"Okay if I make some bets?"

"Bets? Well, yeah, I don't see why not."

Sun Horse nodded.

"But you don't know anything about these horses, do you?"

"What is to know?" Sun Horse asked. "I only need to look at them."

"You're going to pick a winner just by looking at the horses?"

"Yes."

"This I've got to see."

By the time the fifth race came around, Sun Horse had picked four winners.

"This is amazing," Clint said as Sun Horse stuffed a wad of money into his pocket. "How do you do that?"

"You can tell if a horse can run by looking at him," Sun Horse said.

"Yes, but what if they all look like they can run?" Clint asked.

"One looks like the winner."

"Only one?"

"Yes."

"All right," Clint said. "I'm going to bet with you, this race. Let's go and look at the horses."

Clint cashed in on the fifth and sixth races with Sun Horse, but the prices were low. The favorite won each race.

"How about a long shot?" Clint asked him.

"I can't control the price," Sun Horse said, "I can only pick the winner."

"Will you be able to do that in the Derby?"

"Yes."

"You're that sure?"

"Yes."

"All right," Clint said, "what about this next race . . ."

FORTY-FOUR

The winner of the seventh race paid fifteen dollars. It was a good price, and Clint did well. He pocketed the money and said to Sun Horse, "Okay, the Derby's next. Let's go over to the betting windows."

"I have not looked at the horses yet."

"I'm not worried about the winner," Clint said. "I want to be around the windows when the robbery happens."

With no cooperation from Captain Butler in Security, Clint had no idea where all the money went. He felt his only chance to thwart the robbery was to be somewhere the money was—like the betting windows.

He and Sun Horse had just arrived at the windows when Clint saw Captain Butler, a few of his uniformed men, and Sheriff Hackett coming their way.

"Get ready," Clint said.

"I am ready."

"Don't fire unless I do."

Sun Horse nodded.

"All right, Adams," Butler said. "Just stand there. Sheriff, arrest him."

"For what?" Clint asked.

"Trespassin'," Butler said. "Him and all his Indians."

"John Sun Horse and I paid our way in," Clint said. "And the other Cherokee are on the outside. Nobody has broken the law."

Butler glared at Hackett.

"He's right," Hackett said.

"I don't care if he's right," Butler said. "I want them out of here."

"Adams—" Hackett said.

"Don't try it, Hackett," Clint said. "Look, I know you and Captain Butler here are in on the robbery."

"What robbery?" one of the men asked. He was young, and looked smarter than the others.

"Shut up!" Butler said.

"Fontaine is among the missing," Clint said, "and Blacker's dead."

"Dead?" Hackett asked. "You killed him?"

"I did. His body should be sitting in front of your office. I killed him when he came out to the Canby place to kill me."

"You heard him," Butler said, "he killed a man. Arrest him."

Clint looked around as a crowd gathered to watch them. They were taking the attention away from the Kentucky Derby horses, who were coming out onto the track. He also looked to see if he could pick out anybody suspicious, anyone who might be paying special attention to the windows. And then suddenly, a door opened and two security guards came out wheeling what looked like a table on wheels. And on top of that table were bags of money.

"Where are they going?" Clint demanded, pointing.

"They're takin' the money to the vault," Butler said. "What's it to you?"

"The vault?" Sun Horse said. "That is where the robbery will happen?"

"What robbery?" the same young guard asked. "Is there gonna be a robbery?"

"No!" Butler said.

"Yes," Clint said. "But it won't happen until after the Derby. When the betting is all closed and the money has all been taken in."

Butler had four guards with him, but only the young one seemed concerned. Was it possible that the robbers were guards, and were already inside the track? That was Fontaine's plan? If so, then the Cherokee in the outside weren't going to be much help if shooting erupted anytime soon.

Clint was hoping he had time to send Sun Horse out to get them.

"Son," Clint said to the young guard, "I believe the captain, these other men, and also the sheriff are all in on a plan to rob this track after or during the Derby."

"What?" the young man said.

"He's crazy!" Butler said.

Hackett was licking his lips nervously. The other guards were looking toward their boss for a signal.

"Look at your colleagues," Clint said. "They've got their hands on their guns and they're ready to go."

The young guard looked around.

"This isn't—" Hackett started, but stopped short.

"Isn't what, Sheriff?" Clint asked, sensing there was no time left. This was going to be up to him and Sun Horse. "Isn't the way it was supposed to happen?"

Hackett looked at Butler. He said, "Don't—" but it was too late.

Butler yelled, "Take 'em," and went for his gun. The guard followed.

Sun Horse brought his rifle around and fired. Clint drew and fired twice. The young guard pulled out his billy club and brought it down on the arm of one of the other guards, knocking his gun to the floor.

Hackett was down, bleeding from a wound in his arm. Butler was dead, as were two of the guards. The last guard was down on one knee, holding a broken arm. The young guard had his gun out and was pointing it at the sheriff.

"I hope I did the right thing," he said to Clint.

"Don't worry," Clint said to him, "you did."

The people around them had hit the ground when the shooting started, but they were quickly getting up and rushing to the windows to get their bets in.

"They're off!"

Whirlwind went right to the front.

"He will win," Sun Horse said.

"Are you sure?"

Sun Horse nodded.

The other Cherokee were still outside. The guards had been taken away by other guards who had not been in on the plan. The young guard had taken control, and had taken the sheriff into custody. The race went off without a hitch. Wherever Fontaine was, his plan had failed, but he was free to come up with more plans.

For now.

Whirlwind went around the track, dogged every step of the way by Sunday Song. As they came into the stretch, the little colt started to pull away from the larger horse. From behind, Easy Going suddenly started making a move. He was closing the ground between himself and Whirlwind, but by the time they got to the wire, Whirlwind was still a full length in front.

The winner!

"If you had told me that earlier," Clint said to Sun Horse, "I would have bet more."

Watch for

BLOOD TRAIL

381st novel in the exciting GUNSMITH series
from Jove

Coming in September!

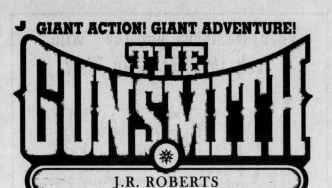

GIANT ACTION! GIANT ADVENTURE!

THE GUNSMITH

J.R. ROBERTS

penguin.com/actionwesterns

M455AS0812

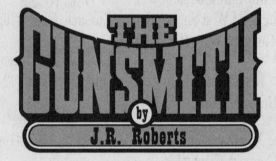
10/14 M11G0610